The Journey features one of the world's master storytellers at work as he skillfully recounts his time as Mexico's Ambassador to Czechoslovakia in Prague and two fateful weeks of travel around the Soviet Union in 1986. From the first paragraph, Sergio Pitol dislocates the sense of reality, masterfully and playfully blurring the lines between fiction and fact.

This adventurous story, based on the author's own travel journals, parades through some of the territories that the author lived in and traveled through (Prague, Moscow, Leningrad, the Caucasus) as Pitol reflects on the impact of Russia's sacred literary pantheon in his life, exploring the inspiration for his own novels and stories, and the power that literature holds over us all.

The Journey is the second work in Pitol's groundbreaking and wholly original "Trilogy of Memory," which won him the prestigious Cervantes Prize in 2005 and has inspired the newest generation of Spanish-language writers from Enrique Vila-Matas to Valeria Luiselli. *The Journey* represents the perfect example of one of the world's greatest authors at the peak of his power.

International praise for Sergio Pitol:

"Sergio Pitol is not only our best active storyteller, he is also the bravest renovator of our literature." —ÁLVARO ENRIGUE on *The Journey*

"Pitol is unfathomable; it could almost be said that he is a literature entire of himself." —DANIEL SALDAÑA PARIS, author of *Among Strange Victims*

"Once again Pitol takes the reader on a transcendent adventure through geography and history. His voice—learned and warm—is the perfect companion on these flights, giving dramatic glimpses into the intellectual life of Soviet Prague one moment and inimitable insights into literature the next. The reader leaves the pages wiser, more enriched and able to fully appreciate Pitol's status in Mexico and the rest of Latin America." —MARK HABER, Brazos Bookstore

"Reading him, one has the impression...of being before the greatest Spanish-language writer of our time." —ENRIQUE VILA-MATAS, author of *Dublinesque*

"Masterful." —*Dallas Observer* on *The Art of Flight*

D1600726

THE
JOURNEY

THE
JOURNEY

—

Sergio Pitol

TRANSLATED FROM THE SPANISH BY
GEORGE HENSON

INTRODUCTION BY
ÁLVARO ENRIGUE

DEEP VELLUM PUBLISHING
DALLAS, TEXAS

Deep Vellum Publishing
2919 Commerce St. #159, Dallas, Texas 75226
deepvellum.org · @deepvellum

ISBN: 978-1-941920-18-3 (paperback) · 978-1-941920-19-0 (ebook)
LIBRARY OF CONGRESS CONTROL NUMBER: 2015935165

—

Esta publicación fue realizada con el estímulo del
PROGRAMA DE APOYO A LA TRADUCCIÓN (PROTRAD)
dependiente de instituciones culturales mexicanas.

This publication was carried out with the support of the
PROGRAM TO SUPPORT THE TRANSLATION OF MEXICAN
WORKS INTO FOREIGN LANGUAGES (PROTRAD)
with the collective support of Mexico's cultural institutions.

—

Cover design & typesetting by Anna Zylicz · annazylicz.com

Text set in Bembo, a typeface modeled on typefaces cut by Francesco Griffo
for Aldo Manuzio's printing of *De Aetna* in 1495 in Venice.

Distributed by Consortium Book Sales & Distribution.
Printed in the United States of America on acid-free paper.

Contents

For Álvaro Mutis,
my brother in Russia

SERGIO PITOL, RUSSIAN BOY
by *Álvaro Enrigue*

There is a story that Sergio Pitol used to often tell when he still led a public life, and which he recorded in *The Art of Flight*. At the beginning of the eighties he spent a two-month vacation in Mexico City, after having lived for years in Barcelona, Warsaw, Budapest, and Moscow. At the time, he was 45 and had six or seven published books; he had translated Conrad and James and had been the editor of the legendary collection *Los Heterodoxos,* published by Tusquets in Spain and with a wide circulation throughout the Americas. Shortly after arriving in Mexico, he received a call from the PEN Club, inviting him to participate in a series of dialogues between writers of different generations—a reading, followed by a public talk, between a veteran author and a novice. He accepted, and they announced that he would read with Juan Villoro. The event almost ended in disaster for Pitol: he thought, as he ascended the stage—twenty-three years and a pile of books older than Villoro—that he was to be the novice at the table. Nothing better describes Pitol's eccentricity: he was a referential figure for an entire literature, and he still thought of himself as a promising writer.

It is this eccentricity sine qua non that allowed Pitol to become first a cult author and then the writer who reintroduced Mexican literature's beautiful secular tradition: authors of genreless books, more disposed to suggest a conversation than impose a monolithic idea of the world through a fiction populated with anecdotes and symbolic characters.

Read in the order published, Pitol's books tell the story of a detachment. The author who began writing spellbinding yet conventional stories about the remote region of Mexico where he grew up gradually shed the themes and languages that gained prestige during the twentieth century: the peculiarity of a regional culture, the relevance of nationality, the Latin American soul in the solitude of exile.

Simultaneous to this detachment—suicide in its time—from the proven themes of regional writing, Pitol implemented a riskier experiment: to shed, too, the superstitions of literary form—or perhaps expand them. Gradually, his books ceased to be novels or collections of short stories or essays, and became literary sessions in which the distance between fiction, reflection, and memory is irrelevant. Books that are everything at the same time—what his contemporary Salvador Elizondo called, half philosophically, half ironically, "books to read."

At the time of the publication of *The Art of Flight* and *The Journey*, the gesture to forswear genre was seen as defiantly postmodern: in order for writing to be total, it had to dispense with the market-related conventions that asphyxiated Latin American literature during the late twentieth century, in which the large publishing houses seemed to have imposed a short-sighted and dull literary taste as the only option for bookstores.

Over time, it is possible to see clearly that while it is true that the acclaim both books received was unexpected, it is also true that Pitol was not acting like a desperate innovator, rather like the attentive reader of a tradition that always found literary genres claustrophobic. Nor did the books of Martín Luis Guzmán, Nellie Campobello, José Vasconcelos, and Alfonso Reyes—founders of Mexico's literary modernity—possess a clear genre. From the same generation as Sergio Pitol, authors like Margo Glantz, Alejandro Rossi, or Salvador Elizondo himself, all brilliant and relatively unknown outside of Latin America, continued to stress that the country's most resilient literary production consisted of writings free of generic conventions.

Sergio Pitol's later books, then, are not capricious. They are grounded in a tradition and are the product of a process in which he has worked in a consistent and serene way over the last twenty years: human experience lacks value until it is transformed into writing; but if the obtuse geometry of genre writing is imposed onto that, its irrational foundation is betrayed. "Inspiration," Pitol notes in *The Magician of Vienna,* "is the most delicate fruit of memory." It is not a new idea: it lies at the bottom of the writing of St. Augustine, Montaigne, and Camus. For the author, the genius that moves literature is correspondence: experience, as Pitol himself says, is just "a set of fragments of dreams not altogether understood."

This is why *The Art of Flight* begins with the myopic description of Venice: in order to see what has value in the world, one must leave their everyday eyeglasses on the desk. The reality is there, but is only meaningful when it is removed by the erasure that implies selecting and assembling a series of episodes, readings, notations. This is also why *The Journey* includes essays, but also diary pages, anecdotes, and stories so circular that they could not be entirely true but are related as if they were. Literary imagination, according to Pitol, does not progress in the rational order that the novel, essay, or short story demand. It is more like a sea sponge than a freeway. It is a solid block, without a basis, but full of inner paths that connect ideas, notes, invented memories.

The beginning of *The Journey* could not be more classic. The author, tired and a bit sick, locks himself away to write in a sort of tropical Montaigne's tower: a modest, cultured, and provincial city on the Gulf of Mexico. He recalls his years as ambassador in Prague and notices that his favorite city of the many in which he has lived is the only one about which he has never written anything. Surprised, he checks his diaries from the time and discovers a hole: they contain only notes about meetings, readings, and petty office problems—not a word about his outings through the never-ending city, its splendid museums, its powerful cultural life. What he does find in his notebooks, however, is a travel diary to Russia that, over time, grew in significance: it records the moment of the Soviet Thaw.

It is here that Pitol's process of writing becomes extreme. His diary is rewritten and edited so that it reads like footage from a documentary filmed at the very moment Perestroika was received by the people of the Soviet Union amid feelings of hope and skepticism. Brought into play by a series of essays on Russian literature, with pages dedicated to the mysteries of the craft of writing and the projection of memories whose connections are not clear until the reader reaches the last line of the volume, the diary produces reverberations that resignify it as it goes along. One must not forget here that the Soviet opening occurred shortly before the transition to democracy in Mexico, which is the precise time Pitol wrote *The Journey*. The year 2000, when it was published, was the same year in which Mexico's long transition toward a system that ultimately guaranteed basic civil liberties ended. His stark mockery of Soviet commissars and his dithyramb on citizens intoxicated by the idea of freedom represent an oblique look at the fiesta that was Mexico in those years full of hope.

But *The Journey* is not a political book—or, rather, it is much more than that. It is framed by three scenes that by reflecting on each other reveal the personal vision of the writing of an author who is at his creative peak. In the introduction on Prague, there is a scene, part terrible and part comic, in which Pitol, wandering the alleys of the city's old quarters, notices an old man sprawled on the ground, unable to get up, who is cursing at pedestrians. When the novelist approaches, he discovers that the man is not drunk, but rather has slipped in his own shit, and every time he attempts to get up slips on it. Later on, when Pitol finally reaches Tbilisi, Georgia, he attends a *supra* given in his honor by an association of writers and filmmakers. He has been, since arriving to the city, in ecstasy: he finds it awake, vibrant, critical, and infinitely freer and more cheerful than Moscow or Leningrad. In that state of excitement, he gets up from the banquet to go urinate and, because the bathroom is closed, one of the guests suggests that they go down to the river to relieve themselves, which is normal.

Having had a little too much wine, he accepts the invitation and discovers a disturbing scene: in Tbilisi shitting in public is not only a socially acceptable act, but also an opportunity to socialize. In the last episode of the book, Pitol returns to his childhood in the tiny town of Potrero, Veracruz, where the entire community earns a living from a sugar mill. Because he was a sickly child, he was prone to loneliness and isolation. One of his favorite outings consisted of getting lost in the mill's naves on Sundays—when it was closed—to reach the place where accumulated huge mountains of bagasse, the unusable crap left behind from the production of sugarcane. There, buried among the vegetable waste, he fantasizes about an illustration from a children's book in which there appears a Slavic child named "Iván, the Russian boy," and imagines himself as his twin. He later confesses that of all the images he has had of himself, that one—the most delirious—is still the one that seems to him "to be the real truth."

The odyssey that *The Journey* relates is not, as it seems at first glance, the one Ambassador Pitol made to the Soviet Union of the Thaw, but that of the solitary child who accumulated faces, names, memories, and turned them into a book. Among the many things included are the notes that the author made to write *Domar a la divina garza* [Taming the Divine Heron]—perhaps his best novel and a truly wild book—which recounts the discovery of a rite of spring in which an entire community in the state of Tabasco is inundated with shit by its inhabitants in an emancipatory paroxysm.

The Journey is at once a lesson in subtlety and in destruction. It is a book that, in order to rescue one tradition, dynamites another.

It is a volume about how a writer constructs. About freedom and its lack; that final, indomitable freedom which is letting go, allowing things to come out: narrating. This is why the book does not function, like almost all the others, as a progressive sequence of stories, ideas, and images, but rather like a hall of mirrors, in which a series of narratives reflect on each other: eschatological tales; a body of essays on the humiliations suffered by Russian writers who chose to pay the price for speaking their mind; a collection of documentary vignettes in which the reader watches live the Soviet generation that was becoming emancipated, fertilized by the sacrifice of those authors and the autobiographical framework of the writer who chose not to comply with any parameters to become who he wanted to be: a Russian boy.

There is a memorable story in the Havana diary with which *The Magician of Vienna*, the final book in Pitol's "Trilogy of Memory," ends: as a young man, while traveling to Europe by boat, Pitol passed through Cuba. One night in Havana he got drunk as a sailor and passed out. The next morning he woke up in his room wearing someone else's shoes, which worried him until he discovered they were Italian, new, superbly cut, and fit him perfectly. For Sergio Pitol everything is in everything and writing is the only way to reveal the secret connections that give meaning to reality. Writing exists so that our shoes fit us.

New York, February 2015

INTRODUCTION

And suddenly, one day, I asked myself: Why have you never mentioned Prague in your writings? Don't you get tired of constantly returning to the same stale topics: your childhood at the Potrero sugar mill, your astonishment upon arriving in Rome, your blindness in Venice? Do you perhaps enjoy feeling trapped inside that narrow circle? Out of sheer habit or loss of vision, of language? Is it possible that you've turned into a mummy or a corpse, without even realizing it?

Shock treatment can yield amazing results. It stimulates weakened fibers and rescues energy on the verge of being lost. Sometimes it's fun to provoke yourself. Without going overboard, of course; I never ridicule myself in my self-criticism; I'm careful to alternate severity with panegyric. Instead of dwelling on my limitations, I've learned to accept them graciously and even with a degree of complicity. From this game, my writing is born; at least that's how it seems to me.

A chronicler of reality, a novelist, preferably talented, Dickens, for example, conceives of the human comedy not only as a mere vanity fair, but rather, he uses it to show us a complex timing mechanism where extreme generosity coexists and colludes in sordid crimes, where the best ideals man has ever conceived and achieved fail to separate him from his infinite blunders, pettiness, and his perennial demonstrations of indifference to life, the world, himself; he will create with his pen admirable characters and situations. With the vast sum of human imperfections and the least—the bleakest, it must be said—of their virtues, Tolstoy and Dostoevsky, Stendhal and Faulkner, Rulfo and Guimarães Rosa, have all obtained results of supreme perfection. Evil is the great protagonist, and even if it is usually defeated in the end, it never completely is. Extreme perfection in the novel is the fruit of the imperfection of our species.

From what delirious alchemy did the most perfect books I know arise: Schwob's *The Children's Crusade*; Kafka's *The Metamorphosis*; Borges's *The Aleph;* Monterroso's *Perpetual Motion?*

Half-jokingly, I managed to convince myself that the debt I owed to Prague was in some way scandalous. I spent six years there in a diplomatic post, from May 1983 to September 1988: a decisive period in world history. I planned to write some reflections on my time there. Not the essay of a political scientist, which for me would be grotesque, but a literary chronicle in a minor key. My conversations with professors of literature, my outings to the imperial spas—Marienbad, Carlsbad—where for centuries during the summer the region's three august courts could be found at the service of their respective majesties—the Emperor of Austria, the Tsar of Russia, and the King of Prussia—along the beautiful avenues where later, from the end of the First World War, time stood still. They are the two largest spas in the region.

To stroll through the streets, among the luxurious sanatoriums, the old hotels built in an era when tourism was not yet accessible to the masses, the elegant villas of the nobility and of the financial magnates, continues even today to be a delight. Plaques abound: on the lavish mansion next to my hotel, where Wagner composed *Tristan und Isolde*; at the Inn of the Three Moors where Goethe summered for several years; on the small theater where Mozart attended performances of *Don Giovanni*; on the hotel where Liszt lodged; at the hall where Chopin played; the apartment where Brahms, and oftentimes Franz Kafka, convalesced from their maladies. There are plaques that indicate where Nikolai Gogol, Marina Tsvetaeva, Ivan Turgenev, Thomas Mann, the Duke of Windsor and Mrs. Simpson, among others, once promenaded. Or to trace Kafka's steps through Prague, from his birthplace to his grave; or to describe the specific characteristics of Prague's Baroque; or the city's vast art collections; or the cultural and social energy typical of the first Czechoslovak republic in literature, in theater, in painting, in society, or on the architecture of the time: the cubic houses of Adolf Loos, the Bauhaus houses built by Mies van der Rohe, and Gropius—in Prague, in Brno, in Karlovy Vary; the bleakness and frustration of the present; the efforts of intellectuals to not grow stale, to not stop thinking, to prevent students from becoming robots; in short, to write a long essay that did not specialize in anything, but that approximated a history of ways of thinking. I needed to review my journals from that time, as I always do before starting any work, to relive the initial experience, the primal footprint, the reaction of instinct, the first day of creation. I read several notebooks, hundreds of pages, and to my surprise I found nothing about Prague. Nothing. That is, nothing that might serve as a basis for writing an article, much less a literary text.

It was—and continues to be—incomprehensible to me. As if one morning I looked in the mirror to shave and could no longer see my face, not because I had lost my sight, but because I didn't have a face. One night I had a dream. I was arriving at a hotel in Veracruz, the Mocambo, I believe. I had taken a room there in order to finish writing a book I had been working on for quite a while, perhaps years; the only thing left was the conclusion. At the restaurant, around the pool, in the gardens, I ran into friends, or rather past acquaintances—windbags, nitwits—with a big smile always on their face and a sycophantic remark always on their lips. I couldn't take it anymore; they were monopolizing my time, so I became insufferable: I talked to them constantly about my novel, told them that for the first time I was satisfied with what I was writing, its development had taken me a long time, too long, but in the end I felt I had finally become a writer, a good writer, a great writer, perhaps. So I couldn't spend time with them, I had to rush to complete the masterpiece on which I was slaving away, I would appreciate it very much if they left me alone while I was there; I went on and on about how wasting my time was worse than stealing my money. Some gave me irate looks, others sarcastic smirks. The day finally arrived when I was able to write the words: The End. What joy! I traveled to meet with my editors, with Neus Espresate in Mexico and Jorge Herralde in Barcelona, or both. I didn't take the manuscript because I needed to iron out a few things first—the contracts, the advance, the release date, I suppose. When I returned to Veracruz, I would give it a final read, have photocopies made, and send them to the publishers. Afterwards: the glory, the celebrations, the medals, the praise, everything that annoys me in real life, but which my unconscious apparently dreams of. Suddenly a storm appears in the dream, then a bolt of lightning, followed by a blackout: I don't know if I came back from the airport to retrieve something I had forgotten, the fact is I hadn't left Veracruz, not entirely, but I was only gone a few hours, and then I returned to the hotel; I rushed into my room and ran—celestial lyre-bearer!—to open my suitcase, to stroke my manuscript, to kiss it. Except there were no notebooks or paper in the suitcase; there were instead huge eggs that suddenly began to crack and from which began to emerge horrible beaks, then bodies, which were even more repulsive, of cartilaginous birds, and I knew, in that strange way that one knows things in dreams, that they were ostriches: a quintuplet hatching of ostriches. I desperately opened another bag and another, out of which sprung ostriches of varying sizes, and the first ones, which I had seen hatch, were now my size, and some were hiding their heads under the bed, behind a door, in the toilet bowl, wherever they could, their droppings all the while falling to the floor and laying eggs wherever they liked. I could have died from despair in that state. I had lost the fruit of many years of work, the work that was going to redeem me professionally, that would lift me out of the mediocrity in which I had always wallowed and catapult me to the summit. I didn't understand anything, and the only thing I wanted was for someone to remove those grotesque fowl from my room so I could lie down and sleep peacefully.

The same emptiness I felt at the end of the dream, when by

bewildering metamorphosis my supposed masterpiece had turned into a flock of ostriches, was repeated in real life when I discovered the complete absence of Prague, the city, in my notebooks. I had lived captive—happily captive!—aware that a miracle took place each time I ventured out into the street and became lost in the network of labyrinthine streets that make up medieval Prague and the old Jewish quarter—my astonishment before the immense panorama that came suddenly into view as I approached the river or crossed any of its bridges; when I slipped into the shade of its thick walls, built and rebuilt throughout the centuries, like palimpsests made of stone and of different clays that contained messages connected to the cult of Osiris, Mantra, and Beelzebub himself. Of all the sciences that found a home in Prague, the one that enjoyed the greatest prestige was alchemy. There was a reason Ripellino gave his best book the title *Magic Prague*. For six years, I visited its sanctuaries, those known to the whole world, but also other secret ones; I wandered splendid avenues that are parks that turn into woods, and also squalid alleys, vulgar passageways, without form or direction. Time and time again I walked rhythmically on cobblestone streets that had known the footsteps of the Golem, of Joseph K., and of Gregor Samsa, of Elina Marty-Makropulos, of the soldier Švejk, of the Rabbi Loew, with a chorus of occultists, newts, robots, and other members of Bohemia's motley literary family. Prague: an observatory and compendium of the universe: an absolute *imago mundi*: Prague.

I was fortunate that my arrival in Prague coincided with an exhibition of Matthias Braun, Bohemia's great Baroque sculptor, who transformed stone, subjected it to unknown tension, extracted from its bosom angels and saints, twisting and arranging them in impossible corporeal positions, and who, in full possession of his liberty, succeeded in making the sacred touch the absurd, the delusional—that which distinguishes the Bohemian Baroque from that of Rome, Bavaria and Vienna. Braun is not a desacralizer, not at all; if anything, he was a man in anguish. I'm ashamed to admit it, but I did not even know until then the name of that great artist. After seeing the exhibition, I traveled the roads of Bohemia and Moravia to see the rest of his work.

I'm almost certain that the same day I allowed myself to be dazzled by the Braun exhibit, I was able to find, with the aid of a city map, the Café Arco, one of the holiest sites of interwar literature, where Franz Kafka met with his closest friends: Franz Werfel, Max Brod, Johannes Urzidil, and the adolescent Leo Perutz. All young Jews from more or less affluent families, writers in the German language, who formed the Prague branch of the Vienna School. They considered themselves provincials, disconnected from the living language, unconnected to contemporaneity, to the prestige of the metropolis, and the truth is that their very existence represented, but at the time neither they nor the world knew it, the zone of maximum tension of the German language. From the street and especially inside, the establishment could not be seamier. It looked like all the bleak and filthy fifth-rate establishments that Hašek created for his soldier Švejk. The same neighborhood where it was located seemed to have lost a former prestige that, on the other hand, must have been modest. Imagining those young geniuses talking around a table in that dreary space, devoid of atmosphere, its floor littered with cigarette butts, greasy pieces of paper, and dirt, exchanging ideas and discussing them, or reading their latest texts to each other, had an obscene quality.

On another occasion, during my first summer in Prague, on an afternoon of stifling heat, I went out, guidebook in hand, to look for a pair of hard to find synagogues and the so-called Faust House. I set out for the latter first, in the heart of the new city. New, in Prague, means anything built after the seventeenth century. The Faust House is a large, solemn, and neutral palace. Not even the blinding light of the summer sun is able to soften its funereal appearance. The house is opposite a square with tall, lush chestnut trees, which, for some reason, fail to enhance the beauty of the surroundings. A tree-covered square, with broad lawns and assorted flowerbeds, devoid of charm. I learned later that once upon a time it was known as the witches' square. As early as the Middle Ages it was believed that sorcerers, witches, spiritualists, alchemists— the very concubines and spawn of Satan!—held meetings on the surrounding premises. Every thirty or fifty years, tempers in the neighborhood flared. Someone would spread the rumor that the corpses of missing children had been found on the banks of the river with marks on their bodies similar to the various signs used in satanic rituals, and so forth, which no one could prove for the simple reason that they had not existed, but emotions ignited, raged, then the expected happened: the doors of slums and hiding places were battered down; the witches and other visionaries were rounded up in extremely brutal fashion; then came the fire that, during the ensuing days, incinerated, fagot by fagot, that accursed vermin that had lost its way. In 1583, the Emperor Rudolf II transferred the Hapsburg capital from Vienna to Prague. His credulity was infinite, and none of the many disappointments he suffered could diminish it. He was convinced that he would find the formula for the Philosopher's Stone, which could extend life as many as three or four hundred years and had already, there was proof, made some humans immortal. He was also convinced that there was an alchemical process whereby a few drops could transform base metals into gold. He claimed to have seen it. During his reign, dozens of alchemists of diverse plumage descended on Prague. The most eminent were granted access to the royal castle, where the monarch enriched them and treated them as equals. However, after a certain amount of time they all met the same fate: ghastly torture, the gallows, the stake, quartering. One of them, Edward Kelley, an Irishman by birth, was the emperor's favorite for many years. Rudolf worshipped him as a second Faust. And for this he gave him the palace, built centuries before by one Johannes Faust, to whom popular tradition attributed fantastic powers of divination, powers he had received, according to popular lore, from the devil himself for having sold his soul. In short, I arrived that hot August afternoon of 1983 to find that the illustrious house had become a hospital. I did not go in; the uninviting façade failed to inspire a visit, nor did I stop at the lackluster plaza that adjoined it—a gloomy continuation of the building. I walked down a street that led to the river. In August, the residents of Prague go on holiday; if forced to remain in the city, they tend to withdraw into their homes and drink beer until the heat subsides. It was a neighborhood unfrequented by tourists. I turned onto an overly modest and poorly cobbled alley. Suddenly, as I walked, I glimpsed a shapeless bundle in the distance on the opposite sidewalk.

As I approached, I saw it move. It was a decrepit old man, with a thick shock of hair, who was obviously drunk. I couldn't tell if he was trying to stand up or squat down. His pants hovered around his knees, a scene as harsh and grotesque as those of Goya. I think as he dropped his pants to defecate, he collapsed and fell into his own excrement. He was cursing loudly and in a menacing tone. No one was passing through the alley except yours truly. I walked past him, cautiously, on the opposite sidewalk; after walking a few meters I could not resist turning my head to look back. The scene was pathetic: with every attempt to pull himself up, the old man would once again fall onto his back; his pants and underwear at mid-thigh acted as a tether, hindering his movement. Even now, I am haunted by the specter of the repeated falls into his excrement and the squeals that sounded like a pig at slaughter. And today, as I write, I still associate that image with a masquerade directed by someone, hiding in the house that belonged to the man who had sold his soul to the devil. And as I think of Doctor Faust, I recall Thomas Mann's book on that character, and that for a number of years, while in exile, Mann was a Czech citizen.

With joy, with spirit, and with boundless curiosity, in a moment of exuberant optimism, I began to feel like a particle of Prague, a poor relative of the cobbles that paved its streets, its erect baroque estipites, its passion, its lights, its defeats, its mire. Why then—I ask myself—in the hundreds of pages that comprise my diaries of that time was there not a single mention of such walks, or the permanent bewilderment with which I attempted to integrate my person into its surroundings?…Was it out of humility? With what words could I describe that never-ending miracle?

What tone would have been necessary to translate into a comprehensible language the murmurs I heard around me and what inclined me to believe that very soon I would succeed in crossing a magical barrier? But what barrier, damn it? In an exemplary essay, Borges reasons that in the Qur'an there are no camels anywhere, for the simple reason that their presence is so mundane that one takes their existence for granted. To mention them would be a pleonasm. The truth is, no answer comforts me. I reread page after page of several notebooks that make up my diary, and I noticed with great consternation that I didn't describe the city in any of them. I seemed to obey a secret order to avoid it, to omit it, to erase it. The most I managed to do was to mention, without even the slightest importance, a restaurant, a theater, a square: "Today I ate at the Alcron with such and such people. The hors d'oeuvres are delicious there. I dare say they are among the best I've tasted in the city;" or "Last night at Smetana Hall I heard Obraztsova as the fortune-teller in *Un ballo in maschera*. We applauded her to death. Much more than the soprano who sang Amelia, who incidentally was also perfect;" or "I just arrived from the airport. I went to welcome Carmen, who told me that it seemed small relative to this ancient city's importance." A restaurant, a theater, the airport. Nothing, in retrospect: twaddle. In contrast, in the same diaries I go on and on about A) the noxious atmosphere I breathed in the foreign ministry; B) the frequent visitors I received from Mexico, Spain, Poland, and elsewhere; what my friends say, what they do, the topics we discuss; C) my physical ailments, medications, doctors, clinics, periods of convalescence in magnificent spas; D) my readings, to which, perhaps, the majority of the space is devoted.

During those years, I returned fully to Slavic and Germanic literature, consistent with the history and creation of Czechoslovakia. I reviewed with almost maniacal voraciousness the authors I had admired since adolescence, and those years in Prague strengthened in a strange, elusive but persistent way, my knowledge of the Czechs. I read all of Ripellino—his books on Russian literature, the Czech anthology, his essays could all be included in the title of one of his extraordinary books: *Saggi in forma di ballate* [Essays in the Form of Ballads]; the Russian formalists, starting with Shklovsky, whose *Theory of Prose* I studied assiduously; Bakhtin's *Rabelais and His World*, which played an extensive role in the novels I wrote in Prague; and massive amounts of Chekhov and Gogol, whom I read and reread at every hour and in every place. During those six years, I also did an extensive review from the Middle Ages to the present of the literature of the German language, the most historically influential in the lands of Bohemia and Moravia, especially its Austrian variant. I found myself closer to Kafka than in any previous reading. As I frequented his daily haunts, I felt closer to his visions. In my youth, my enthusiasm for Kafka transformed, as happened to my entire generation, into a true passion, with all the exclusivity, visceralness, and intransigence that implies; it was equivalent to the first moment in which one feels overpowered by a spirit that he recognizes as undoubtedly superior, the only one capable of explaining in depth a time that will never disappoint us. In Prague, his role grew immensely. It was not merely a matter of providing the scope of an era, but of knowing the whole universe, its rules, its secrets, its ways, its purpose. The signs for knowing the answer are hidden in his writing; they must be sought in earnest.

I set my sights on two other fascinating figures: Thomas Bernhard and Ingeborg Bachmann, both Austrians.

The hatred of the Russians was intense, monolithic, visceral; and no fissure, not even the slightest nuance, was allowed. It extended, albeit with less intensity, to the other socialist countries for having collaborated in the military occupation that cut short the experiment known as "socialism with a human face" in Prague in 1968. When I arrived to assume my post at the embassy, fifteen years had passed since this despicable event, but the memory of the tanks in the streets, the days of humiliation and powerlessness, the absurd argument that the Czechs and Slovaks had requested assistance to put an end to the enemies of socialism redoubled the population's anger rather than assuage it. In the city center, there were two spacious Soviet bookstores always teeming with people. But no Czech or Slovak would set foot in them. The feverish horde that crowded inside to reach the shelves before others emptied them with exorbitant purchases consisted of Russian tourists or travelers from the other Soviet republics, who as soon as they arrived in the city, rushed to bookstores to acquire art books and literary editions that in their country sold out immediately, due to reduced printings of works that differed from the official canon, or those that touched on "dangerous" topics, which in Moscow could only be purchased with hard currency from the West, which when purchased in Prague with Czech korunas were a steal. Appearing in these collections were Anna Akhmatova, Marina Tsvetaeva, Mikhail Bulgakov, Aleksey Remizov, Andrei Platonov, Isaak Babel, Osip Mandelstam, Boris Pasternak, Ivan Bunin, Boris Pilnyak, Andrei Bely, and other writers persecuted by Stalinism—enemies of the people, cosmopolitans who had turned their back on the nation, the recalcitrant bourgeois, those who were executed, those who spent long years in the Gulag; others, who were treated better, who lost the right to publish their work during long periods of their life, those who began to reemerge after the death of Stalin, were vindicated and over time became the greatest artists of their century, literary classics, and notable examples of human dignity. Russians came to Prague in the morning and returned to Moscow at night, just to purchase dozens of books they would then sell in Moscow or Leningrad at prices so exorbitant that they could make a profit even after traveling by plane. Near my embassy offices there was an exclusively Soviet press office, which no one ever entered. From time to time I would pause in front of its windows and not once saw anyone buy a newspaper or magazine. On television, one could easily watch a Soviet channel with less banal programs than the national ones, and I would even venture to say less ideologically rigid. As always happens, of course, to win the trust of superiors, these programs had to brim with ideological zeal, be more Catholic than the Pope. Once a week, on Saturdays, I occasionally watched masterfully directed and acted plays on this channel, to which I had grown accustomed from when I lived in Moscow. But if I mentioned it in the presence of my Czech friends, they grew silent, pretending not to have heard my comments, as if they suddenly suspected a trap.

The absence of written references to my day-to-day contact with Prague discouraged me. On the other hand, in one of my notebooks, I found an envelope with notes on a short trip I had made to the Soviet Union during the Gorbachev experiment.

As I read these notes, I recalled moments of irritation and moments of pure emotion, constantly interspersed with each other, during the two weeks I spent in the bosom of that empire that had taken centuries to forge and whose impending collapse neither I nor anyone else could foresee. I got the idea to rework those notes, to set aside the texts from my diaries and to mention briefly, by way of background, some situations about my experience in the period in which I worked as a cultural advisor in Moscow.

Upon arriving in Prague, I looked for a Russian teacher, and a Czech woman came highly recommended; I read literary texts, practiced conversation with her in the language, and we did translation exercises. She was retired, which allowed her a freedom of movement that many others lacked. No one could expel her from anywhere for approaching a diplomat, nor could they remove her pension. Like all Czechs, she felt the wound of history in her marrow; she no longer believed in the possibility of a revival of socialism. When news began to circulate that a relatively young Communist leader in Moscow was trying to ease international tensions and introduce in his own country liberal reforms, among others an easing of literary and film censorship, she laughed sarcastically. She had heard it so many times, and everything always stayed the same if not worse, "Surely this is a ploy," she said, "to fool Americans and to try to take advantage of them." Some time passed, almost two years, I think, and one day she came to our lesson rather upset with a copy of *Ogoniok*, a Moscow magazine detested by all of my acquaintances in Moscow. "A friend of mine, who is also a teacher," she said, "brought me this magazine; I've read it from cover to cover, and I've barely been able to sleep since.

I still can't believe it, but the fact is that something serious is happening on the other side of our border. Revolution! Not even in '68 did they write things like that here." We began to work that day on a very well written article about Meyerhold's final days of freedom and the monstrous persecution to which he was subjected at the end. The help of Eisenstein, one of his best friends, to save his archive and a few documents, if the worst were to happen. The article ended with the chronicle of his arrest as well as different versions of his death and the prison camp to which he had been sent.

By this time, I was not only watching the Soviet channel on Saturdays for the theater programs; I was also following the daily newscast. And every week I would stop by the Russian newspaper store, which was no longer the desolate space it once was, to pick up a copy of *Ogoniok*, which I paid for in advance because it usually sold out within a few hours of arriving. *Ogoniok*! It seemed inconceivable that *Ogoniok* had been rehabilitated, had become decent! For many years it was a weekly. During the Khrushchev period, it became a publication of monstrous intolerance, of a repressive police mentality. It was headed at the time by Vsevolod Kochetov, one of the organic writers of Stalinism, a mediocre novelist, primitive to the point of exaggeration. After that leech, even more powerful reactionary forces followed, linked to the repressive apparatus. Kochetov ferociously insulted the intellectuals of the Thaw, the old ones because they dared to say what they had kept silent for so many years, the young ones because they expressed themselves disrespectfully and without fear. The target on which he unleashed most of his animosity was the magazine *Novy Mir*, and its director Aleksandr Tvardovsky, who dared to publish some of the literature that had been banned for a long time, among other things Solzhenitsyn's *A Day in the Life of Ivan Denisovich*, a novel that caused an unbelievable uproar. Kochetov disappeared shortly thereafter and plunged into personal and literary infamy. His primitivism and vileness did him in. When he spoke of the Jews he did so with the language of the pogrom; the hardliners demanded more cryptic individuals to continue, but more efficiently, what the former barbarian said. The *Ogoniok* that I read in Prague was a brave, fresh, modern, well-written publication. It had taken on the task of cleaning up the Stalinist as well as recent past, the economic and political paralysis and corruption of the immediate past. When I read an issue, I sensed a breath of oxygen that triggered in me an enormous sympathy for what was happening in the Soviet world. Compared to the Czech Plateau, its lethargy, its passive fatalism, this was an invitation to life and, in my case, a stimulus for creativity.

Later, when what happened and the way it happened passed, I found in Elias Canetti's autobiographical notes a few lines with which I feel a deep kinship:

> Orphans—all of us who wagered on Gorbachev, half the
> world, the whole world. For decades, I never believed
> so strongly in anyone, all my hopes were pinned on him;
> I would have prayed for him—I would have denied
> myself. But I am not ashamed of it at all.[1]

1   I have been unable to locate either the English translation or the original quote. The only reference to the quote in Spanish I found was in an article

At the end of the day, I'm not going to write about Prague, I'll do that later, but that magical city led me to other excerpts from my diary: to the country of great achievements and horrific turmoil.

It was an unexpected trip. In early 1986, four years after my arrival in Prague, I unexpectedly received an invitation from the Union of Writers of Georgia to visit the republic in May. Georgia had suddenly become famous because of the subversive nature of its films, and was regarded as one of the strongholds of perestroika, the word that denoted the transformation initiated by Mikhail Gorbachev in the USSR. I was invited to spend a few days in the capital Tbilisi and its surroundings as a writer, not as a member of the Foreign Service, not to participate in a conference, nor to celebrate a centennial of a national hero. I accepted, of course. I began to recall things. A strip of contemporary Georgia was once the famous Colchis, the homeland of Medea, that long-lost place where Jason and the Argonauts arrived in quest for the Golden Fleece. A few days later, the Ministry of Foreign Relations informed me that the Ministry of Culture of the USSR was extending an invitation for me to travel to Moscow from the 20th to the 30th of May of that year. They requested a lecture on some aspect of Mexican literature, which I was free to choose. The invitation came from the Union of Soviet Writers. I assumed it was in response to the letter from Georgia, so that the world would know that it was the metropole that continued to decide when

titled "Delayed Effects" in *La Jornada Semanal*, April 13, 1997, where the quote is attributed to Canetti's "notes from 1993." (I have endeavored to cite existing English translations of all quotations. In some cases, I was unable to locate either the original source of the quote or an English translation. In such cases, the translation is mine. —*Trans.*)

and to whom invitations were extended and that everything else was a vague and wide-ranging peripheral space.

From the moment I arrived in Moscow, I began to inquire about my departure to Tbilisi, but the bureaucrats who welcomed me avoided the question; they would change the subject, or at most they would say that they were in contact with their Georgian colleagues to establish my travel schedule. "You have lived here and know how the Caucasians are, people from the South, friends of the sea, of the sun, but much more of wine and celebration, they lose track of time, we know them very well and so do not worry. In the end, they work everything out," and they added that in the meantime they would be my hosts, and were pleased to assist me in Moscow and Leningrad, a city they had not mentioned until then. Then, in Leningrad, I was informed that the Georgians were devastated that they were not able to welcome me, because as is always the case in spring, tourism exceeds all possibilities of accommodation. They should know because they had already had embarrassing incidents such as this, but that's how they were, pleasure-seekers, people of the beach, sun, wine. Nothing rattled them, they were happy people, pagan, yes, good at dance and singing, no one was better, with a wild imagination, an ancient and refined folklore, but definitely careless, chaotic, irresponsible, even dangerous in some ways, one could say… They proposed that I go to Ukraine instead of Georgia. Compared to ancient Kiev, Tbilisi was little more than a picturesque village, they said. I knew that Ukraine and its capital Kiev were extremely beautiful places, but I also knew that in recent decades its cultural institutions were the most resistant to any social, political, or aesthetic change, and that the arts in that republic continued to follow the strictures of socialist realism from 1933, directed by unimaginative, mediocre, and unscrupulous party officials.

I was about to cancel the trip. Apparently, a game of equivocations had begun, which I no longer wished to play. I had all my luggage ready, so I left for the airport, believing that I would go to Prague, but instead I went to Tbilisi. And, despite the bad omen, the trip was wonderful. I witnessed something unique: the first steps of a dinosaur that had been frozen for a long time. There were beginnings of life everywhere. It was a consecration of their spring, celebrated amid thousands of obstacles, traps, faces marked by hatred. Something of that, I hope, will be translated into the notes that I was able to scribble on airplanes and buses and in cafés and hotel rooms.

Two hours into the flight and the feeling of having forgotten, as is always the case, things I will need during the trip. Mrs. A., a television official, whom I run into frequently in airports and on airplanes, and also at diplomatic receptions, suddenly changed places and came to sit beside me. From that moment on, she talks non-stop. It's the same every time I see her, and no matter what we're talking about, she manages to change the subject, always to the same one, which, apparently, obsesses her. She travels frequently, attending film and television festivals in Spain and Latin America. She loves to talk about her trips and her experiences; she almost always is besieged by brutish and impatient hot-blooded men who give off a smell of sweat and from whom she only manages to free herself with great difficulty. By the end of the episode, she grows demure, contradicts herself, blushes, so her listeners will draw a more unchaste conclusion. I am certain that if given enough rope, she'd lower herself to the bottom of the pit, wallow in the muck with delight, her own intimate confidant, relishing those episodes of a strictly sexual nature. Undoubtedly she has repeated these unpleasant and tiresome confessions many times before, because her speech is mechanical, dispassionate, devoid of even a hint of eroticism. After weeks of perfect health my rhinitis has returned. I didn't sleep well last night, nor did I did finish packing, so today I had to wake up early in order to finish. I had a dream on the plane: I was at the Posada de San Angel about to leave, saying good-bye to some friends. Suddenly, Mauricio Serrano, a classmate from university, walked by and stopped to talk to me. I said to him, "I read recently that you had died in an accident, is it true?" (And yes, of course it was, I had read that the actual person, whom I call here Mauricio Serrano, had died in an airplane accident. His private plane had crashed in the Chihuahua or Sonora desert, I don't remember which. We were classmates in law school. He was very thin then and extremely tall. I remember him as one of the first students who attended classes without a tie but in very elegant sportswear, which at that time was almost a provocation. I must have only talked to him four or five times in my life, and about nothing, the weather, even less. We belonged to different worlds. I knew he had made a lot of money, but I don't remember how.) The dead man, without answering me, walked toward another group. Minutes later, on my way to the bathroom, I saw him again, leaning against a tree, a pine tree I believe. I suggested that we go have a drink somewhere. We made the rounds of several bars, but no place would let us in, as if they sensed something was wrong. In the few places that did let us in, the dead man ordered dozens of limes, which he sucked on desperately. I guess he needed them to maintain his simulacrum of life, so he sucked them furiously, as if he were afraid to enter a state of putrefaction.

We arrived in Colonia Juárez, to a building on Calle Londres where I lived for several years in my youth, in such a way that made the trek very long. The inside of my apartment was the same as before, except that the walls were bare, without any of the wonderful paintings from before. The dead man began to bore me, to annoy me, he did everything possible so he wouldn't have to leave. It seemed as if he had something to tell me, but he didn't know how, as if he had a message for me, perhaps that I would die soon, a greeting from the other world, something, anything, but everything he said was trivial. His vocabulary was very limited, his topics of little interest. I felt the same irritation that has always produced in me a cloud of termites against which I have fought all my life to protect my time. Finally, when I succeeded in getting him to leave, his color was frightening. "I won't be able to last without decomposing, no matter how many limes I eat," he said as he left. I woke up suddenly; I thought that the dream was real. No longer seeing the fireplace in my old studio and to be sitting instead in an airplane seat gave me a terrible shock. But only for a moment. Had Serrano been a messenger from the other world? Had he conveyed his message in such a hermetic way that—because I was distracted or because all I could think of was getting rid of him—I was unable to grasp it? My dream must have lasted an instant, because the functionary hadn't even noticed. Drunk with conceit, she was telling me how the three Brazilian actors who accompanied her in San Salvador, plus a Cuban boxer, had at the same time pulled out their penises in a garden, in front, behind, and on both sides of her, and begun to urinate without a single drop—she was intent on making this point clear—touching her skirt, like mascarons shooting their streams toward the center statue of a fountain.

Hours later

In Moscow, near the city center. The city imposes its urban design on me, its spectacularness and power. "Moscow is the third Rome, and there will not be a fourth," is one of the Slavophil slogans from the sixteenth century, which has governed the Russian subconscious ever since. How wonderful to drive along Gorky Street! It was enough just to arrive to perceive the change. There's discussion about the new political moment, the new plays, the new cinema, and the new problems that everyone faces: the new, the new, the new against the old seems to dominate the present moment. Shortly before landing, Mrs. A. confided in me the repulsion that the changes in the Soviet cinema cause her. "Irresponsibility can cause disasters," she said, "and these people are not ready for such changes; they need to be educated first, if not they'll create problems. The Georgians are the worst, the least reliable. They've made a one hundred and eighty degree turn, which means turning their back on their rich cultural tradition; they would curse it if they could, erase it. Their social criticism is too strident, ridiculous, crude. Nothing good can come of it, as you will see." I accept these displays of rancor with absolute bliss. Then, from here, from the hotel, I began to call my friends, I sensed their enthusiasm. My encounter with the city is so strong that I can't write anything coherent about it. I walked more than three hours without stopping anywhere. Tomorrow afternoon, I'll read my lecture on Lizardi and *The Mangy Parrot* at the Library of Foreign Languages. I feel overwhelmed. Worse than that: I try to put images from the past in order, but I'm not entirely able. That night, I see the filmmaker Nikita Mikhalkov on television, speaking openly with the audience. Yes, gentlemen, the world was beginning to move! It's midnight. The only thing I feel like doing is going out again, to the bars I know well. But I won't. Instead, I'll take a very hot bath and go to bed with Jules Verne's *Michael Strogoff, or The Courier of the Czar*. I'm returning to his pages after forty years. I know, it's peculiar to arrive in Moscow with Jules Verne, but I couldn't help myself.

20 MAY

I woke up with a cold; my head kills me at times. I get by with aspirin, and that has allowed me to do many things today. I recall my first visit to Moscow in late 1962, during a harsh winter, they called it the winter of the century, and I believed them. Later I heard of at least a dozen colder winters of the century in Eastern Europe. Those were the days of Khrushchev. I hear the same kind of hopeful talks again then sense the same fear that the apparatus, the army, the police agencies, the *nomenklatura,* and—let's be honest—the apathy of the people will annihilate what has already been done and close the doors to the future for a long time. The Arbat, the picturesque old quarter, where Pushkin's house still stands, not far from our embassy, is an active example that winds of change are blowing: cafés, restaurants, young people dressed in brightly colored clothes, with guitars and books under their arm. They tell me that a carnival was held here for the first time in Moscow since the 20s. It was organized by young people who dressed in masks and costumes of their own making; the festival turned out to be so entertaining that the people of neighborhood were speechless, no one imagined that this could be possible. It seems insignificant, but for fifty years young people lacked

possibilities as simple as that, except members of the Young
Communist League, who at different levels, whether by geography
or guild, organized public activities, but always with a civic purpose: day of the teacher, of the woman, of the athlete, fiftieth
anniversaries or centennials of the birth or death of a leader of
the labor movement, a hero, or a historical event. Young people
were left with other possibilities for escape: the cult of friendship,
sex for some, religion for others, culture for many, but above all
eccentricity. Faced with centuries of cruelty and an unrelenting
history, against the robotic nature of contemporary life the only
thing they have left is their soul. And in the Russian's soul,
I include his energy, his identification with nature and eccentricity.
The achievement of being oneself without relying too much on
someone else and sailing along as long as possible, going with the
flow. The eccentric's cares are different from those of others—his
gestures tend toward differentiation, toward autonomy insofar as
possible from a tediously herdlike setting. His real world lies
within. From the times of the incipient Rus', a millennium ago,
the inhabitants of this infinite land have been led by a strong hand
and endured punishments of extreme violence, by Asian invaders
as well as their own: Ivan the Terrible, Peter the Great, Nicholas
I, Stalin; and from among the glebe, among the suffering flock,
arises, I don't know if by trickle or torrent, the eccentric, the fool,
the jester, the seer, the idiot, the good-for-nothing, the one with
one foot in the madhouse, the delirious, the one who is the despair
of his superiors. There is a secret communicating vessel between
the simpleton who rings the church bells and the sublime painter,
who in a chapel of the same church gives life to a majestic Virgin

greater than all the icons contained in that holy place. The eccentric lends levity to the European novel from the eighteenth century to the present; in doing so, he breathes new life into it. In some novels, all the characters are eccentrics, and not only they, but the authors themselves. Laurence Sterne, Nikolai Gogol, the Irishmen Samuel Beckett and Flann O'Brien are exemplars of eccentricity, like each and every one of the characters in their books and thus the stories of those books. There are authors who would be impoverished without the participation of a copious cast of eccentrics: Jane Austen, Dickens, Galdós, Valle-Inclán, Gadda, Landolfi, Cortázar, Pombo, Tomeo, Vila-Matas. They can be tragic or comical, demonic or angelic, geniuses or dunces; the common denominator in them is the triumph of mania over one's own will, to the extent that between them there is no visible border. Julio Cortázar creates a kind with which he constantly plays: *los piantados*, the nutcases, those characters outside the constraints of the world, with two registers, one of a genius and the other of a simpleton. There are authors and characters whose eccentricity in this time of yuppies would have led them to a cell in an insane asylum or a retirement home with medical treatment if their finances allow it. The world of the eccentrics and their attendant families frees them from the inconveniences of their surroundings. Vulgarity, ungainliness, the vagaries of fashion, and even the demands of power do not touch them, or at least not too much, and they don't care. The species is not characterized solely by attitudes of denial, but rather its members have developed remarkable qualities, very broad areas of knowledge organized in an extremely original way. Dealing with friends of this kind can at first be irritating, but little by little it develops into an unavoidable necessity. To the eccentric, other people, from outside his circle, are difficult, pompous, pretentious, and insufferable for a thousand reasons; so he chooses not to notice them. Some fifty years ago, during our first years at university, Luis Prieto and I circulated within a network of cosmopolitan groups dominated, sometimes in excess, by eccentricity; many of them were Europeans who came to Mexico during the war, who found here the promised land and did not return to their countries of origin. We moved among them with remarkable ease. When an unrepentant sane person fell into those spaces, a close relative, for example, who was visiting from abroad, a mother, a brother, whom it was impossible to not host or entertain, that sane person in a sane person's clothing became unbearable; even to those of us who were not part of that brotherhood, but were merely fellow travelers, his presence in that environment seemed insane, but despite this, one made all the necessary concessions, the same ones that they, the sanest of the sane, would do when they are generous and well-mannered for someone with a mental problem. Of all the places I have lived, only in Warsaw, but especially in Moscow, was I able to become part of those enchanted spaces, those hives of "innocents" where reason and common sense wane and an "odd" temperament or mild dementia may be the best barrier to defend oneself against the brutality of the world. The mere presence of the eccentric creates an uneasiness in those who are not; I have sometimes thought that they detect it and that it pleases them. They are second-rate "oddballs." My stays in those cities considered difficult by most of the world were for me welcome refuges of unspeakable happiness, always conducive to writing…Everything surprises me here. Is it possible that the time has arrived in which the truth is beginning to break through—or is it another illusion? I think it wouldn't be bad at all to spend a long while in Moscow, within the next four or five years, if by then this phenomenon takes off and senescence hasn't gotten the best of me. I have breakfast with my friend Kyrim. He summarizes the Congress of Filmmakers, which took place last week: the Association's leadership was replaced completely. It has been an explosion of national proportions. None of the dinosaurs of the old guard remained in their posts, including some extremely powerful and prominent figures from a professional point of view like Sergei Bondarchuk, director of *War and Peace*, a true classic of contemporary Russian cinema. He lost his job due to his sectarianism, his contempt for the trends of young people and contemporary forms, and for trying to keep alive that abhorrent maxim coined by Siqueiros, no less: "Ours is the only path." I understood better the concerns of my seatmate from the plane; if what happened here occurred in Prague, the film studios would be closed and she would be discharged from her post. No more festivals in San Sebastian or Latin America! The tropical men, the mulattos, their spectacular pricks would disappear from her fantasies, and she would be constrained to local experiences. I should have started this entry with Kyrim Kostakovski, a mathematician, but fundamentally a man of the cinema. He was at the National Film School of Lodz at the same time as Juan Manuel Torres, and was married to a Mexican, one of my best friends. Years ago, I traveled with them to Tashkent, Bukhara, and Samarkand; I wrote one of the few stories of mine I like about that trip.[2] We had not seen each other for five or six years, but from the first moment, we began to talk like always, as if no time had passed. As with all my Russian friends, I would discuss with Kyrim film, literature, opera, people, and, of course, politics, until the wee hours of the morning. I often decided that I was no longer going to tolerate his irascible outbursts. Our dialogues resembled those of Naphta and Settembrini: each of us began to defend a play, a literary movement, a type of cinema—Bergman's, Fellini's, Clair's, or Pabst's—and the other would insult it until late into the night and with wracked nerves each of us would end up defending the position that he had previously attacked and refuting what he had originally defended. In other words, arguing, whether for hours or days, is a Russian sport. Kyrim's passion for Gogol, vast and unfailing, is perhaps what most unites us. Over the years and distance our dialogue has become much less strident. After recounting to me the circumstances of the film conference, he told me that he had accompanied Viktor Shklovsky to England. The University of Essex had awarded him an honorary doctorate. After the ceremony they returned to London, where they had been booked in a rather mediocre hotel. No expense had been spared on the public events, banquets, social activities, etc., but when it came to lodging the British really cut corners. They had planned a to visit to the British Museum in the afternoon. The writer was about to leave his miniscule cubicle when, after making a sudden movement to open a door, an armoire fell on him. He rolled to the floor under the cabinet; the

---

2   The story to which Pitol is referring is "Nocturno de Buhara" [Bukhara Nocturne]. —*Trans.*

blow caused him to lose consciousness. A doctor arrived, applied iodine and arnica, gave him an injection and, with considerable trouble, managed to get him into bed. Shklovsky is a man of eighty-five, if not older. Kyrim thought that because of his age he might not survive the blow. Devastated, he returned to his room to rest a moment, waiting for another doctor to arrive, a specialist who had been called. Half an hour later, he heard the phone; he feared that it was the hotel manager or the new doctor with bad news. But no, it was Shklovsky himself, ready to head to the museum. They spent the rest of the day there, touring its many rooms, seeing everything, collecting data, taking notes, theorizing. Only on the plane back to Moscow did he begin to complain of discomfort, and he showed Kyrim his purple-blue swollen ankles. Kyrim's grandfather met Shklovsky in his youth, back in the twenties. He was a mathematician and supporter of the October Revolution. In 1937, uniformed men came to their house and took him away; shortly thereafter, three of his sons were kidnapped. They were Jews and Trotskyists—therefore, enemies of the revolution, agents at the service of foreign espionage. Kyrim's father was the only survivor, having been at the time barely a child. In 1957 the honor of the entire family was vindicated, but none of them returned from Siberia alive. He and his family have been rather skeptical. But this time Kyrim is excited about what is happening in the country, especially in film, and tells me that wonderful films have been made and about what is on the horizon: Abuladze and Paradzhanov in Georgia, he says, are fabulous, and he tells me about a Russian film by Gelman, in his opinion the best in the history of Soviet cinema: *My Friend Ivan Lapshin*,

"A very sad film, the farewell to an epic, a sentimental story about all the wretched generations who have lived in Russia in this century." Try to see it here, he says, because in Prague you will for sure never be able to. The public, of course, is divided; the intelligentsia, students, scientists are all in favor of this kind of cinema, but we are a country of masses, immense masses manipulated from above, guided by emotion, and they will undoubtedly think it's an insult to our history. In the afternoon I gave my lecture at the Library of Foreign Languages: "Fernández de Lizardi and *The Mangy Parrot*, the First Mexican Novel." A small audience, a handful of Hispano-Americanists, mostly friends or acquaintances from my previous stay; one of them, in a very fraught Spanish, paid me very nice compliments in his introduction, but said he was glad to see me again in a Moscow freed from the defects that caused me so much pain in the past. Who knows what he meant! After the reading had begun, the door opened noisily, and a woman of an advanced but difficult to discern age, tall, stout, dressed elegantly in black, marched in and sat on the front row, directly in front of me. She listened to me with indifference, like a Roman matron who for some unknown reason had to endure a reading by one of her slaves. And so she remained throughout the whole lecture: haughty, histrionic, commanding attention, except at the end, when I read a scatological fragment that I introduced as an example of a language that broke ties with the legal and ecclesiastical language used until then in books. An effort to find the language appropriate to the circumstances of the new nation. This episode takes place in a disreputable gambling house where the protagonist seeks shelter for the night:

33

Four or five other wretches, all in the buff and, as far as
I could see, half drunk, sprawled like pigs over the bench,
table, and floor of the pool room.

Since the room was small, and our companions the sort of
people who eat cold, dirty food for supper and who drink
pulque and *chinguirito*, they were producing an ear-shatter-
ing salvo whose pestilent echoes, finding no other outlet,
came to rest in my poor nostrils, thus giving me in one
instant such a migraine that I could not bear it, and my
stomach, unable to withstand the fragrant scents, heaved
up everything I had eaten just a few hours earlier.

The noise that my evacuating stomach made woke up one
of the *léperos* there, and as soon as he saw us, he started to
spew a blue streak of abuse out of his devilish mouth.

"You raggedy sons of bitches…!" he said. "Why don't you
go home and vomit on your mamas, if you're already so
drunk, and not come here to rob people of their sleep at
this time of night?"

Januario signaled to me to keep my mouth shut, and we
lay down on the billiard table; and between its hard planks,
my migraine, the fear instilled in me by these naked men
whom I charitably judged to be merely thieves, the
countless lice in the blankets, the rats that ambled over
me, a rooster that spread its wings from time to time,

the snores of the sleepers, the sneezes that their backsides produced, and the aromatic stench that resulted, I spent the most miserable night.[3]

The woman on the front row lost her stonelike expression. When I referred to "the snores of the sleepers, the sneezes that their backsides produced, and the aromatic stench that resulted," she shouted, filled with passion, "That, gentlemen, is the Mexico that I love!" And then when I asked if anyone wanted to ask a question or make a comment, she was the first to speak. "Coincidence of coincidences!" she said. "I came to the library to find some pamphlets written by my husband, Adam Karapetian, the anthropologist, deceased now unfortunately for twenty-five years in Medellín, Colombia, where I live, Armenian by birth, of course, as the surname implies. They are all studies about your country, inspired under the stars, written first in 1908 and again in 1924. On the latter date I accompanied him to the jungle. I was about to leave the library just now when I saw the announcement for a lecture on Mexico, yours, *maestro*. If my husband were alive he would have stood up to embrace you, because you both work along the same lines I can tell. I'm looking for those opuscules, some very difficult to find, they don't have them in this library, but I am sure I'll find them where I least expect it. The most important one concerns a feast in the tropics, a religious feast with a pagan end. Karapetian was only interested in the feast as an anthropological topic, the feast in Mexico, Bahía, Puglia, New Guinea, Anatolia. The one that most interested him was one in the middle of the Mexican jungle in honor of a holy shitting child. (Laughter.) No, one mustn't be afraid of words, what one must consider is in what circumstances the feast was celebrated. I was there, I saw it all! The blazing sun and the land transformed into shit! It took twenty days for my nose to lose that stench!" And then she got up, put a card in my hand and left the auditorium with an air of extreme dignity. As the door closed we all broke out into laughter. The card read: MARIETTA KARAPETIAN, and below the name the inscription: FINE HAND PAINTED CHINA and, then, another line in tiny, almost illegible print read: I APPLY LEECHES. HYGIENE AND DISCRETION GUARANTEED. Who knows what that could be! I still haven't met the translator of my novel *Juegos florales* [Floral Games]. I was hoping to talk to her after the conference, but she didn't introduce herself. I'd love to walk around for a while, but I'm afraid of the dampness. I wouldn't want to wake up with another cold tomorrow. Tonight I'll finish *Michael Strogoff*, and then go to bed.

The night before last, when I arrived at the hotel, a young man was waiting for me to hand deliver a very formal invitation from Georgi Markov, president of the Union of Soviet Writers, to lunch with him and other distinguished members of that institution on May 21, that is to say today. This morning, while eating breakfast, I ran into the same person. The first thing he said was that something terrible had happened. The Mexican ambassador had accepted the invitation days ago, but had suddenly cancelled, and sent word that he had another commitment at the same time. The young man asked me to try to convince him; with his presence, the ceremony would acquire greater importance. I told him, in a very cordial way, that none of that mattered. "In the invitation sent to Mexico, you noted that my visit had no official status; I was not invited as an ambassador nor as an official but as a writer. And I am very grateful for that gesture. What interests me most is literature." "Allow me to inform you," he interrupted, "that President Markov is the host. He rarely attends these events. His position, as you know, is of the same rank as Minister of Culture, surely you remember. The ambassador will have to attend.

I can take you to the embassy." "But how can you expect me to make that request? Did you not tell me that he has another engagement at that time?" "That is what he said, but we know he does not have another engagement. He will not tell you…" "No, look, I can't help you. It would be an unforgivable impertinence. He is a very busy man, extremely busy, one of the busiest I know and I do not want to interrupt him. What interests me is to talk to the writers; rather, for them to tell me what is happening, what is being written now, what their readers think. In Prague there is enormous enthusiasm for this process. The government engages in self-criticism every day and every day there are new results. A Resurrection, thanks to your country." Of course this was not true, in Prague the authorities were desperate. There was almost no mention of the USSR in the press or on television, but I could not resist the temptation to lie parodically. He wrinkled his face and returned to the charge. "What you are asking me to do is impossible," I said. "I am an ambassador, but this is not my post, and the ambassador in Moscow could report me to Mexico for interfering in a sphere that is rightfully his. Do Soviet diplomats do things like this? You are the ones who can convince him. Talk to him politely, tactfully, why not ask the cultural attaché to intervene and convince him?" He left, and while I was finishing breakfast, he returned and said: "Your embassy's minister, as chargé d'affaires, will represent the ambassador. Thank you for the suggestion." We said goodbye. At noon, someone was coming to pick me up. I went out to walk the Gorky for a while. I read with interest the billboards of several theaters in the area. I bought newspapers at the Intourist, especially those from Italy, which cover this area better than any others, and returned to my room to make some notes. I have never met any of the high-ranking leaders of the Writers's Union. Never was Markov present, not even when an important delegation arrived, Juan José Bremer as Director of Bellas Artes or Fernando Solana as Secretary of Education. I went several times to the Union's restaurant, with the ambassador, a friend of many years, Rogelio Martínez Aguilar, who was interested in all aspects of that society, and fortunately in the world of culture in particular. Rogelio, as ambassador, was entitled to reserve a table there and invite writers, musicians, and filmmakers. I remember one occasion when he and his wife invited a married couple who were specialists in Mexican culture: Vera Kuteishchikova, a literature researcher, and her husband, Lev Ospovat, who had just published a biography of Diego Rivera, and me. The dining room was more animated than usual, normally there was no conversation at the tables, but they seemed to be unusually energized because of a literary scandal that had erupted a week or two before. A group of prominent writers, the most important of whom, if I remember correctly, were the poets Andrei Voznesensky and Bella Akhmadulina and the novelists Vasily Aksyonov, perhaps Fazil Iskander and Bulat Okudzhava, had edited a literary almanac. When the volume appeared a storm erupted. The Party ideologues considered it repugnant. Mikhail Suslov, the Torquemada of the Central Committee, expressed his rejection: in no way did that literature reflect the Soviet image; quite the opposite, it portrayed a decadent and perverted world. For neglecting the ideological aspect, the hammer fell on the Writers' Union, whose leadership redirected it fiercely against the implicated writers. They threatened the youngest ones with branding them as pornographers. In every newspaper and magazine, articles appeared with the usual cowardice, letters to the editor, all written following the same model, expressing astonishment, horror, anger, disgust, at the poisonous fruit of that nest of stateless degenerates who published their malignant writings at the expense of the money of the working people. The differences (if any) were minimal between a pensioner from Arkhangelsk, a retired military official from Leningrad, an engineer in Baku, a group of construction workers in northern Moscow, a photography club made up of widows on the island of Sakhalin, a few teachers from Odessa, a club of hunters from Omsk, a cell of pioneers from an island in the Arctic: all demanded the authorities take action on the matter and impose the appropriate punishment on the group of outcasts. There were of course punishments, two of the youngest, those labeled pornographers, if I remember correctly, were expelled from the Writers' Union. Vasily Aksyonov resigned his membership in the Union and went into exile. The aforementioned evening when the Martínez Aguilars invited us to dinner, a couple entered suddenly: a still attractive woman of a certain age, with a beautiful smile, on the arm of a young man who looked more like a Hollywood heartthrob or famous athlete than a writer; we were all susceptible to the surprise caused by the appearance of the couple there. There was a moment of silence, followed by a brouhaha and frenetic movement. Vera Kuteshikova told us that the woman was Bella Akhmadulina, the former wife of Yevtushenko. The poet paused to greet a few friends, while attendees at several tables rose to pay tribute to the couple. I imagine there must have been faces full of hate, but I don't remember seeing any, it certainly wasn't the rule. "Was she not one of those implicated in this recent literary scandal?" Rogelio asked: "She seems not to be worried, does she?" And Vera responded, "What does she have to be worried about when she's holding hands with Georgia's Minister of Culture?" Then she and her husband explained that Georgia was becoming a sanctuary for Russians from Moscow or Leningrad. "Painters, scriptwriters, playwrights, anyone worthwhile can find protection in Georgia. But that the Minister of Culture himself would come to the Writers' House to support a woman who has fallen out of favor is unheard of. I think Akhmadulina has roots in the Caucasus, in Georgia certainly; it is a way of protecting her." "But why in Georgia?" I asked. "Because the Georgians are the most formidable people in the world," she replied, "even though they can also be worse than the devil, we Russians know that very well." I enjoyed the venue immensely. It was the former Palace of the Rostovs, yes, the same Rostovs of *War and Peace*. One of the best scenes in Bulgakov's *The Master and Margarita* also takes place there, precisely in that restaurant; Walter Benjamin dined there frequently during his stay in Moscow. On subsequent occasions, I was invited by writers and translators, or by employees whom I befriended, like Yuri Greyding, from the Spanish-American section, who on numerous occasions took me to little known neighborhoods of old Moscow or to visit writers he thought would interest me. On one occasion, we spent the morning, which I recall as one of the most remarkable of my life, in the house of Viktor Shklovsky, where he, with his more than eighty years, spoke passionately about the book he was writing at the time, *Energy of Delusion*,

"The one I have most wanted to write, and has given me the most·
pleasure," he told us, and then he talked to us at length about the
morning Tolstoy died, when he was a student in Petersburg. The
press has been ordered not to publish anything, not a single line
about his death in the papers. Shklovsky walked out his front door
and suddenly saw people vanish, businesses were closed in a matter
of seconds, the carriages stopped. There was a majestic, sacred
silence, as if the world had died, as if the earthly globe had stopped
in its orbit, and then, suddenly, everywhere there appeared an
inconsolable weeping multitude, ill with mourning, orphaned
because their father had abandoned them. The churches had closed
their doors so no one could enter; Tolstoy had been excommu-
nicated many years before. But the crowd surrounded them,
drowned them, rendered them trivial before the mighty oak that
had fallen, the earth had died and Russia was in mourning. My
visit with Shklovsky is one of the most intense, most lyrical, most
exciting moments I can remember. Much later, on two occasions,
when speaking of Tolstoy to my students, I began to repeat Shklovsky's words, but I could not finish them. My eyes welled with
tears, my voice cracked, and I had to take out my handkerchief
and pretend to blow my nose, clear my throat, blaming it on
a cold, allergies, because it seemed grotesque to announce the
death of a Russian writer and start to cry. They arrived for me at
one-thirty. For years the Union has been run by a handful of
Stalinists, cynical, obtuse, and rapacious. They serve as the armed
wing of the Party leadership. Having said that, almost every writer
and translator is listed as members of the Union: the good, the
bad, the terrible, the noble, and the vile. I was received by the *capo*,

an elegant man, very European, some sixty-odd years old, along with five "writers" whose names I did not know. We waited for over half an hour for the minister from the embassy, killing time, talking about the weather, my experiences in Moscow as a cultural advisor, my travels at the time through some Soviet republics. They were all very convivial, but were annoyed by the delay of the Mexican diplomat. The time came when we went into an elegant private dining room in which I had never entered, we drank various kinds of vodka, all excellent, and like birds of prey we swooped on the delicacies—the *zakuski*—that the Russians devour as a prelude to the actual meal. A waiter removed the plate of the absent guest. Several details indicated that my prestige had fallen through the floor as a result of not being accompanied by any embassy official. Markov did not even hide his contempt; he barely spoke, and only indirectly, to his people, on matters related to the Union. I think when I said something he yawned. The others asked me about my favorite writers: I mentioned Gogol and Chekhov above all, then Tolstoy, Bulgakov, and Bely. They made the obligatory comments—expendable and interchangeable—and fired off the appropriate quotes. Then, suddenly, there was movement, a young woman came in—it was the Mexican cultural attaché, apologizing for arriving late and bearing greetings from the ambassador, from the minister, from the entire staff of the mission of Mexico. The *capo* forced a cold smile, greeted her soberly, and gave her the cold shoulder throughout the meal. Little by little we inched toward the elephant in the room. I feigned absolute innocence, I treated them as if they were key agents of change and they shared my enthusiasm with equal zeal.

I congratulated them. "It's a big change, the whole world applauds it. The Soviets' decision to take such a decisive step toward openness is being celebrated on Czechoslovakia and all over Europe. The Czechs informed me that your Union has played a significant role in the transition." I continued talking, as if sure that perestroika and glasnost were their doing; as if they felt that the changes that had taken place would make their lives fuller, their work more productive, and their literature, their beloved literature, their true *raison d'être*. Not a single muscle twitched in their faces. I added that yesterday in Moscow I had heard that they were on the eve of a conference of the utmost importance, which would undoubtedly be as important as the one the filmmakers had held recently. The director was evidently furious, the others looked at each other, puzzled, not knowing what to say. Markov finally responded to my provocations, saying that in the USSR cinema and literature inhabit different spheres, their infrastructure is not the same, nor is their space of reception. Russian literature did not require transformations, it was very rich in form and in content. Foreigners had managed to introduce germs of debauchery, distortions, a cloud of dangerous anarchy to the country; but fallacies like these would not prosper at any time. "Of course," he underscored with emphasis, "we do not defend the anachronistic, society would not allow it; we are current, we know we must be, but in our own way and not that of others who think they know better than we what we need." Now truly furious, he added, addressing the writers present, as if reprimanding them, that fortunately the Ukrainian delegation would be the largest at the Conference, so he was sure that Soviet literature would never be defeated, that it would maintain its dignity, its noble mission, its commitment to the nation, as in its best moments. And with that we stopped drinking our coffee, he stood up, said goodbye with distant civility and left, accompanied by three of his retinue, who were so outraged that they did not even extend their hand as they said goodbye. The other two escorted us to the door. One of them told me that he had written a book on Gogol and that he found it interesting that a Mexican was so enthusiastic about him, the most Russian narrator of all. "About Dostoevsky, Tolstoy, and Chekhov one could understand: they are so very Russian, of course, but their problems are universal. Gogol is also, but less obviously so; he's like a snail stuck to the most recondite wall of the Slavic labyrinth. The best book on Gogol is Bely's," he added. "He published it in 1933, it was a miracle that it appeared even then, the year in which socialist realism became indispensable, and the book by Bely, fortunately, was completely the opposite, an explosion of imagery, discoveries. Hopefully," he added, "now that taboos are beginning to fall the book will reappear." We parted on friendly terms. I imagine that these two members of the leadership will not join the Ukrainians. I took a nap. I woke up depressed; perhaps I was too rude. If someone is invited to eat and accepts, he should be polite. If someone participates in a conference, a symposium, a roundtable, then he is entitled to say what he thinks, even if it proves to be annoying to others. But then I remembered Markov, those career inquisitors, profiteers, petty tyrants, the heirs of those who tortured and killed Babel, Pilnyak, Mirsky, Mandelstam, the great man of the theater who was Vsevolod Meyerhold, and persecuted Pasternak horribly, and Akhmatova and Platonov and so many others, and I felt a sense of satisfaction for having said what I said, and I thought it was not enough. Perestroika is beginning to work on me.

Between 1933 and 1939 hundreds of thousands of citizens suspected of terrorist activities were arrested throughout the Soviet Union as enemies of the people: some were Trotskyists, others agents of intelligence services in Europe and Japan. Among them, in the early morning of May 16, two intellectuals of great importance were arrested: the writer Isaac Babel, whom we all know, and the theater director Vsevolod Meyerhold, Russian theater's greatest innovator. Meyerhold was to the theater what Eisenstein was to film.

During the final phase of perestroika, a committee of writers led by Vitaly Shentalinsky began, after a tireless and arduous struggle with police agencies and their defenders, the inspection of the literary archives of the KGB. These documents are horrendous and shocking; the whole of the terror of the Great Purge is encapsulated there.

Those arrested, in general, were convinced that top state officials did not know what was happening in the country, that their imprisonment was the result of a provocation organized by perverted minds to discredit the Communist system, and carried out by murderers of the worst sort.

The far-reaching purges began in December of 1934, after the assassination of Sergei Kirov, a member of the Central Committee of the Communist Party, whose popularity obscured the figure of Stalin. During the Gorbachev period, people began to speak openly about the possibility that the murder was arranged by the NKVD and ordered by Stalin himself. The persecution of the enemies of Kirov brought an end to all of his opponents. "We must extinguish the enemy without quarter or pity, without paying the slightest attention to the moans and sighs of professional humanists," a senile and troubled Gorky demands in *Pravda* on January 2, 1935. The systematic work of extermination, the so-called "purges," decreased in late 1939. One of Gorbachev's great virtues has been his attempt to clean up the past. Communism would be devoid of any moral grounds if it did not vigorously reject the crimes committed. Khrushchev was heroic in denouncing Stalin's crimes, releasing political prisoners falsely accused and restoring their reputation when the whole of the mechanism of terror was in motion, when the criminals were still alive. The apparatus took a few years but eventually halted it. Gorbachev is attempting to take the next step. The old guard has placed in his way the same obstacles—adding even more—with which they defeated Khrushchev. They made the task impossible for him; they caused him to fail. And what they achieved was a suicide. Times were different and they, oblivious to reality for a very long time, succumbed and destroyed what was left of the socialist system.

In Vsevolod Meyerhold's file, Shentalinsky found a letter to Vyacheslav Molotov, president of the Council of the People's Commissars, with the assurance that if it arrived in his hands he would be released and, also, the criminal proceedings being employed in the Lubyanka would end.

> The investigators began to use physical methods on me, a sick, 65-year-old man. I was made to lie face down on the floor and then beaten on my feet and spine with a rubber strap. They sat me on a chair and beat my feet from above, with considerable force…For the next few days, when those parts of my legs were covered with extensive internal hemorrhaging, they again beat the red-blue-and-yellow bruises with the strap, and the pain was so intense that it felt as if boiling hot water was being poured on these sensitive areas. I howled and wept from the pain. They beat my back with the same rubber strap and punched my face, swinging their fists from a great height.

> When they added the "psychological attack," as it's called, the physical and mental pain aroused such an appalling terror in me that I was quite naked and defenseless. My nerve endings, it turned out, were very close to the surface on my body and the skin proved as sensitive and soft as a child's. The intolerable physical and emotional pain caused my eyes to weep unending streams of tears. Lying face down on the floor, I discovered that I could wriggle, twist and squeal like a dog when his master whips it. One time my body was shaking so uncontrollably that the guard escorting me back from such an

interrogation asked: "Have you got malaria?" When
I lay down on the cot and fell asleep, after 18 hours
of interrogation, in order to go back in an hour's time
for more, I was woken up by my own groaning because
I was jerking about like a patient in the last stages of
typhoid fever.

Fright arouses terror, and terror forces us to find some
means of self-defense.

"Death, oh, most certainly, death is easier than this!" the
interrogated person says to himself. I began to incriminate
myself in the hope that his, at least, would lead quickly to
the scaffold...[4]

VSEVOLOD MEYERHOLD

---

4   Translated by John Crowfoot.

22 MAY

Morning at the Pushkin Museum. I lingered in the hall where the Matisses are, both upon entering and on my way out. To see them again is like winning a prize. I wanted to go later to the little Gogol Museum. It was in that apartment where he spent his last crises, it was there that he burned the notebooks written over the years, including the second part of *Dead Souls*, where he spent his long death throes and lived his last scene, pathetic and grotesque like everything having to do with him. The priest who tortured him for months, Father Matvey, a cruel and demented mind, had attached a cluster of leeches around his nostrils (to extract the bad blood and the fetid mucus he was emitting); as he lay dying, he regained consciousness from time to time, during one of which, quite disturbed, he tried to wrest the disgusting animals from his face, horrified because he believed that the fingers of the devil were seizing his soul. He died with that conviction, and he was right, except the devil's name was Matvey, but he did not know it. The place is small, I seem to remember it having sparse, rundown furniture, all of it from the period of Gogol, which may have even been his. I couldn't go in because it was under renovation.

I only went there once, when I worked at the embassy, accompanied by Kyrim. There were about seven or eight of us at the time plus the old woman in charge of explaining the author's life, his work, and his belongings; we all began to act like characters from Gogol, as if someone had hypnotized us or wound us up. It was not an intellectual or student audience. They were people of modest means; one would think they only came to a museum because they were one step from the door and a terrible storm suddenly struck. But that was not the case. I spent about half an hour there, maybe more, fascinated by the nonsensical conversation that arose among the small group of spectators and the director, from all appearances the only employee, with that look only old maids possess: fragile, trembling, sophisticated, and modest, a caricature of expressions and gestures of Marlene Dietrich and Kay Francis, a voice that whistled trying to hide the absence of an upper front tooth; the others, as far as I remember, were a hearty and cranky old man, another man of the same age, timid and skittish, and a young deaf-mute, a girl his age, perhaps his girlfriend, who translated the director's explanation into sign language, and two older women who moved like wind-up dolls, without blinking or breathing, but alive, that was immediately obvious. I think that was all of us. The little old maid recounted inconsequential episodes from the life of Gogol, coloring them with a moralistic and didactic tone; she transformed him into a "positive" writer, "realist in form and national in content," "as progressive as they come." The timid old man dared, in a terrified voice, to ask if his influence had reached the October Revolution, and the other old man, the sour-faced man, who from the outset had assumed command, roared: "*Vaprosi patom!*" (Questions at the end!). Whenever Kyrim would translate into French for me something I did not understand or when I made a comment to him, the grumpy man looked at us ferociously and demanded respect for Russian culture and for the revolutionary work of the immortal hero whose house we were in. Another time, the same old man chided the young woman who was translating into sign language the old woman's speech for the mute to be discreet, and to try not to attract attention with so many gestures, because it amounted to a boycott of culture. For a few minutes there was a tension that wasn't particularly threatening. It was clear that the situation would have to lead to a comic end, which we began to provoke covertly. Upon hearing us speak French, the spinster attempted to demonstrate for our benefit knowledge that she was seldom able to display. All of a sudden, she said that Gogol wrote standing up just like Hemingway, so that his blood would better irrigate his scalp and fantasy would flourish like in an apple orchard. The splenetic man wanted to know who the person was who wrote standing up, and the woman, with mocking courtesy, replied that it was none other than Hemingway, an American writer and friend of the Soviet Union. "Answer, citizen, why have you compared him with Gogol?" And she, vindictively, responded with the *Vaprosi patom!* that the old man had abused until then, and she continued sketching the image of Gogol, but it was no longer at all "positive:" she referred to the young writer's first trip abroad, when after landing at Hamburg he wrote to his mother that he had left Russia to cure a venereal disease, a terrible clap, difficult to cure in St. Petersburg, only to, at the end of the same letter, recant and ask that she never believe the fallacy that his enemies were spreading in Saint Petersburg, discrediting him to the world and especially in the eyes of his revered Pushkin so that he would abandon him in disgust. "Citizen, you are going too far in your insolence, be careful, I am warning you, you would do well to reconsider," but the horse was already out of the barn, and she commented that some of Gogol's contemporaries, during his years in Rome, insinuated that he was a reprobate, not because he was afraid of women, that was the least of it, but because he was marked by terrible obsessions, such as falling in love with dying youths, whose bodies were marked by an almost immediate death, without which there could be no explanation for the marvelous creations of such a mad genius, and she stopped. We all applauded enthusiastically. The irascible old man started kicking the ground. He opened a door and said: "I demand, citizen, that you confess what it is you are hiding here," and at that moment the deaf-mute pushed him, and the two middle-aged women, who had not said anything, closed the door. We all ran out of the house-museum to the building's central courtyard. The young woman asked for help from a doorman who approached us to remove the madman from the museum. We then saw the bizarre man ranting to himself, without any of us under-standing a word. The timid old man was questioned, and said that the irate man had launched into the director and threatened to harm her if she continued to clarify for us the life of Gogol and of other Russian writers, that all he wanted was for her to tell him about an American writer who wrote standing up, to which the two women bore witness, and the madman was ordered to not cause any more scandals in public places, and to be thankful that at that hour of the day there was not a *militsioner*, a policeman, because if there had been, he would see how it would have gone for him to threaten that noble old woman, the custodian of Russian culture. As I write, I think I may be exaggerating, that everything happened very quickly, very routinely, crazier and more Gogolian, much funnier, and not as pretentious and sensationalist as I described it. Questions at the end! I had lunch today at Baku with diplomat friends, midlevel career officials, two of them specialists in cultural affairs. Baku is one of the best restaurants in Moscow, with food and music from Azerbaijan, a different crowd than other places, many Caucasian faces, especially Georgians. I felt as if I were witnessing a reenactment of conversations about perestroika with diplomats in Prague. Livelier, of course, because we were at the center of events. The host is a Brazilian friend, Antonio, an art connoisseur and collector, widely read, the son of a professor of aesthetics; I have shared two posts with him but only for a short time, as one of us was leaving the other was arriving; I was bound to him more by a taste for letters more than to other diplomats with whom I have dealt in different cities over the years. Angelo was there, also "cultured," whom I met years ago in Hungary at the Italian Cultural Institute in Budapest, and whom I ran into again upon my arrival in Prague. He left a few months later; I could not imagine him in Moscow. I am indebted to him for having introduced me to two writers who have been fundamental to me. In Budapest, he spoke to me enthusiastically about a young Austrian and his works and presented me with a copy of *Gargoyles* in Italian, it was my first contact with Bernhard; and in Prague, on my arrival, he told me that the key to understanding the culture of Bohemia lay in Ripellino, his namesake—Angelo Maria Ripellino—whose *Magic Prague* he also sent me. Someone at the Mexican embassy mentioned in passing that I was going to spend a few days in Moscow and suggested to Antonio, the Brazilian, that he invite me to lunch. The reaction to world events is largely a matter of biotypes: the pessimist, the skeptic, the optimist, the person who knows that everyone around him is naïve (to avoid a cruder term), the person who believes he is the only one who possesses the truth, the person who is not interested in anything, the scholar, the slacker, the sensualist, the surly, and so on. They say that from week to week the situation here changes, that internal alliances split frequently, other unpredictable ones emerge, and there are provocateurs among the higher ranks that create panic among the masses. There has been a conspiracy to allow food to rot in the fields and not reach the cities, to prevent trains and airplanes from departing on time and wages from being available on payday. One would think that decades had passed, but in reality it was just two years ago that Gorbachev began to cautiously introduce new terms into the official discourse. At that time the Baltic republics were the best allies, and there are now conflicts with them. Forces are being dangerously radicalized. In some sectors, there's a feeling of enthusiasm, at universities especially, among the intellectuals, but in others the resistance is stunning. The country could come to a halt with a general strike by the miners. A number of writers who during my time moved within the liberal sphere, in important positions, such as Valentin Rasputin, the Siberian, have become frightened by the pace of change; Rasputin believes that Western influence is excessive, and he has partnered with a despicable group. Like he, there are others who during the times of Khrushchev passed for liberals and are now the opposite. Some of the diplomats at lunch do not trust Gorbachev, nor the possibility that something serious is happening in the country because they think he's a fraud, that he's hiding behind a libertarian façade to confuse the West, he's trying to get the Americans to be careless so that by the time they notice they'll have already signed documents on disarmament that threaten the whole world; or because he knows very well that perestroika cannot succeed because the Russians are not educated for freedom, they do not want it, it is not a part of their culture. Deep Russia will reject all the changes because the sacred element here is essentially pagan, pantheistic: land, forest, vast rivers—Nature remains the greatest deity; Gorbachev knows all this very well, but the national excitement serves to get rid of his opponents. At every turn, there is an official who falls, a powerful politician who goes on a long technical assignment to the Arctic or as ambassador to Africa. Once he has gotten rid of all of them, he will forget about democracy, about uncensored creation and will become a czar like all the rest. I heard these and other arguments. When lunch was over, my Italian friend, Angelo, says that he never imagined he would live in such a formidable moment as this, touch history with his hand. I told him about my conversation yesterday with Markov at the Writers Union, about the Ukrainian bloc that could halt any changes. "Indeed," he says, "they are nervous, what happened with the filmmakers has them on the edge of hysteria, they never thought that something like this could happen. No one, absolutely no one, could foresee that Bondarchuk would have to go home with his arms up in the air, not even the rebel filmmakers themselves. Perhaps the writers will not take such important steps in their conference, but they are sure to gain a widening of their creative space. If the hardline literati prevail, God forbid, they will have to make more concessions than there were during your time. Sure, they'll make noise, they'll threaten, they'll seem more intolerant than ever, now that their slogans are atrocious, they express them crudely, as if Stalin and his gunman Zhdanov had risen from the dead, but that is just lip service, I suppose. They have lost a great deal of power." That evening, Gogol again, this time at the Sovremennik, a perfect theater, a superb performance of *The Government Inspector*. When the Russians are good at theater, no one surpasses them—they are supreme. Khlestakov, the false inspector general, is a dissolute young man, an imbecile and a trifler, as demanded by the text; this performance could have been merely a very amusing sketch, and that would have been fine, but this staging takes on a remarkable complexity, it becomes a game of chiaroscuros while remaining immensely entertaining. The presumed inspector, despite his apparent insignificance and vacuousness, is the incarnation of evil. In the first scene, he appears subordinate to his servant without even realizing it; his birdbrain does not allow it. Khlestakov is anemic and colorless, non-existent; the footman, on the other hand, is decisive and active. He is the brain and Khlestakov his instrument, a puppet molded out of clay. He acquires whatever shape the other characters impress on him; he obeys reflexively, changes colors immediately, the words he speaks are those the listener longs to hear. He is the voice of his master, and the master is Osip, the servant. In this staging, the almost psychopathic aspect of their relationship is accentuated, and a climate of terror that any *don nadie,* any nobody, can cause in his surroundings. We are witnessing a world terrorized by a grotesque lunatic, a straw doll, manipulated like a marionette, a two-bit Golem. In the theater lobby, there is a large photograph of Khlestakov in a 1926 staging executed by Meyerhold. The actor was named Erast Garin; he is characterized and dressed in a ridiculous and macabre way, an expressionist figure, similar to the character Conrad Veidt in *The Cabinet of Dr. Caligari*. It reminded me for a moment of a brilliant production directed by Erwin Axer in Warsaw of Brecht's *The Resistible Rise of Arturo Ui*, where he demonstrates how a band of gunmen invents a *capo* and transforms him into the absolute ruler of a State. The scenery shows a world crowded with yellowed bundles of official documents, torn and stained with fly droppings that add a bureaucratic stamp to the terror. The pacing is brilliant, rapid, delirious. The name of the formidable young actor who plays him is Vasily Mishchenko. A good while has gone by, I'm in my room, but I seem not even to want to leave the theater. Tomorrow I fly to Leningrad.

FAMILY PORTRAIT I

> *Ah, how far translated by now, how abstracted,*
> *Marina, are we even at heartmost pretext.*
> *Signal givers, no more.*[5]
> RAINER MARIA RILKE

I've spent the last few months reading Marina Tsvetaeva. Among my Russian books I have editions from Moscow from 1979 and 1984; all of the Spanish translations, owed to the passion of Selma Ancira; the Italian ones prefaced by Serena Vitale; her poetry in French; and a large volume of English prose with an introduction by Susan Sontag; as well as the biographies by Anastasia Tsvetaeva, her sister; Simon Karlinsky; and Veronique Lossky. I began to acquire them several years ago; however, I had only read fragments, without any continuity. I became familiar with her name during the years of the Thaw, the period that followed the revelation of Stalin's crimes. Ehrenburg in his memoirs underlines her importance in Russian poetry and becomes her shadow council, like those of Mandelstam and Babel, to republish her works and exhibit them to a generation that knew nothing of her journey through life and of the splendor they introduced into the language. During my stay in Moscow I was present at endless meetings where there was always someone debating until late into the night the enigmas her life and family attracted. Whether it was true that in her final

---

5   Translated by Walter Arndt.

days in Moscow, during her years as an exile, an outcast, she had
met with Anna Akhmatova, and if so, what happened during those
visits, what they talked about, in what tone, with what results.
Some said that during a long walk through the woods, on a winter
afternoon, wrapped in woolen shawls, Akhmatova recited from
memory her *Requiem*, while Marina moved her lips and hands
pretending to be talking, or arguing about something, to confuse
professional witnesses. Others argued that those evenings meant
nothing, that Akhmatova feared Tsvetaeva, that she was aware of
her harsh temperament, her arrogant recklessness, so the only two
times they met, she stayed on the defensive, treated her politely,
because she was a true lady, and also with compassion because
of her tragedy, because her heart was immense, and so everyone
gave different but always complimentary versions for Akhmatova,
a woman beloved by all, and swore that they came from absolutely
reliable people: the doctor of one of them, or a friend of Anastasia,
Tsvetaeva's sister, with whom she shared her house, or a teacher
who knew them both, and could spend whole nights listing the
loves that Tsvetaeva was known to have had, and how disastrous
she could be in that regard, a pest, a pain, because of the persecution to which she subjected beautiful young men who admired her
as a writer or for her unique personality, for everything genuine
there was in her, but could not and would not respond to her
demands because they had a different sexuality that placed them
in impossible situations. And they could go on about this topic to
infinity because some of my friends were students of theater and
had been students, and somehow also friends, of those who half
a century before had been the ephebes who were targets of the

excessive libido of that intrepid Amazon. And if one spoke of the Efron family, of Marina, of her husband Sergei, of Ariadna, the daughter who had just died around that time (when I worked in Moscow), of Mur, the son, it was a never-ending event. One of the biggest mysteries that surely no longer is, since one can check the archives of the KGB, is why, if Sergei Efron, her husband, was an important agent of Soviet espionage, as some say, he always lived with his family in a poverty that teetered on beggary. I had read poems in anthologies of Russian poetry, a story or two and many articles about her. At the insistence of Selma Ancira, I began to read the great poetess this year; I began with the press proofs of a 1929 book on the painter Natalia Goncharova, whom she had just translated, and I have continued reading her to this day.

The next book in my reading marathon was *A Captive Spirit*, recently published by Galaxia Gutenberg, in Barcelona. The most important essay in the book is a splendid portrait of Andrei Bely, written in 1934 when she learned of the death of the celebrated author of *Petersburg*. Tsvetaeva's writing in the thirties attained a remarkable distinction and her prose was absolutely original; every essay from her pen becomes a search for one's self and its surroundings, which in itself is not new, but the formal treatment, the certain and bold narrative strategy is. She invents a different discursive construction. In her writing of this period, the thirties, always autobiographical, everything dissolves into everything, the minuscule, the jocose, the digression on the task, on what is seen, lived, and dreamt, and she recounts it with unexpected rhythm, not without a certain delirium, an alacrity, which allows the writing itself to become its own structure, its reason for being.

A Captive Spirit is the perfect example of this type of essay that she wrote during her final years; it consists of the creation of an atmosphere—incomplete portraits—she is not interested in creating biographies—few details, more or less tics, eccentricities, digressions on writing, her surroundings, fragments of conversations, a sense of montage as effective as Eisenstein; nothing seems important, but everything is literature. The friendship between Bely and Tsvetaeva was brief, a few months, no more than two or three, in the dynamic Berlin of 1922, while Marina awaits her husband whom she has not seen in seven years, who is to come for her and take her to Prague where he is studying philology at the Charles University. Bely implored her to get a room near his, because Berlin depressed him, he feared dying, it brought him bad memories at all hours, his wife had run off with someone disgraceful, he said, she had left him forever, and he did not dare return to Moscow, since before leaving he had burned all bridges forever, so a return could be dangerous, fatal. Tsvetaeva got the room, but he did not receive her letter because in his desperation he had returned to Russia, whence he never left. Tsvetaeva was infuriated by this false step, without realizing that she would do the same, in worse circumstance and, of course, with fatal results.

The Tsvetaeva editions, as well as her biographies, are illustrated with photographs of the writer and the other *dramatis personae* who surround her. To see the faces of the characters in this tragedy, throughout the temporal circumstances, means reading a much deeper writing. The first photo that appears in *A Captive Spirit* is the one I prefer; it is of an elegant couple, with an inner harmony that illuminates the figures and landscape.

The characters are sitting on the grass in a forest possibly near Moscow. It appears to be well into autumn or the soft start of winter. They are wearing heavy coats, woolen scarves, and head coverings. At that moment it is evident that they are happy; this can be seen in every inch of the photo, certainly because they are together in that beautiful forest, I imagine, and, above all, because they have reunited once again in their home country, which they had abandoned many years ago. They are father and daughter, Sergei and Ariadna Efron, the husband and daughter of Marina Tsvetaeva. The date of the photo is 1937, when the daughter decided to return to Moscow to work at a news agency, and also the year in which Efron arrived, months later, fleeing the French police that believed him to be involved in a political crime. Not a shadow of care can be seen in the photo that brims with happiness: a sheer idyll. There was even less of a glimpse of the tragedy that was soon to rain down on them. During the moments of that happiness, Marina Tsvetaeva and Mur, her young son, remain in France in desperate economic conditions, friendless, homeless, surrounded by a general hostility. Two years pass and the family finally reunites in a village just outside Moscow. Two months later, Ariadna is arrested and later sentenced to eight years of hard labor in Siberia; a few days later Sergei Efron suffers the same fate, but his sentence is harsher: capital punishment. The family's pro-Marxist element disappears unexpectedly, and not in enemy space, but in what is supposedly their own. In contrast to Marina, the aristocrat, who has written elegiac poems to the White Guardsmen, who is planning a collection of poems in which she will sing the greatness of the tsar's family, the enemy of the Bolsheviks, escapes unscathed;

but she is unprotected in Moscow, with appalling economic difficulties, in a world of terror, where many of her close friends have disappeared, also kidnapped by the political police. The Prince Svyatopolk-Mirsky, her friend, the most subtle historian of Russian literature, the first who praised her abroad and thereby attracted the tribal hatred of Russians in Paris, also returned to the homeland and converted to Marxism, disappeared like her daughter, her husband, and her sister Anastasia, of whose support she was certain. Some other friends are in danger, their homes have been seized, and they cannot help her. She does not understand anything. She assumes, as do all Russian exiles in Paris, that any intellectual who did not openly fight the government possessed special powers in the interior. The World War arrives; the Germans cross Soviet borders. The chaos is immense. Marina and her son move from one small room to another in an increasingly precarious Moscow. Georgy, her beloved Mur, whom she has treated all her life as a mere extension of her body and spirit, rebels: he accuses her of having destroyed his father and sister due to thoughtless attitudes, a lack of tact and arrogance; such that, they would also most certainly be killed soon. This is the harshest blow. That son who had always been wrapped in cellophane not to be touched, not even by air, rebukes what little intuition she has left to survive; he badgers her, makes her responsible for having done everything that should not have been done. Indeed, they do not survive, Tsvetaeva eventually commits suicide in 1941, and Georgy is sent to a boarding school for children of enemy parents of the country, he later joins the army and marches to the front, where, of course, he succumbs, it seems in 1944. Of them only Ariadna survives and endures eight years with unimaginable courage in a concentration camp. In 1948, after completing her sentence, she is released, only to be arrested again months later and sentenced to live for the rest of her life in an atrocious region of northern Siberia, in a climate where the temperature falls to fifty degrees below zero, where she survives another six years, to be rehabilitated on the death of Stalin. In subhuman conditions, Ariadna begins to establish, from a place that does not even exist on maps, contact with relatives and friends of her mother, contemporary writers, publishers, editors, whoever might have knowledge of the whereabouts of her mother's papers. Before returning to Moscow, Tsvetaeva had deposited in a Swiss literary institution some folders with writings that could endanger the family—political poems in praise of the Whites: *The Demesne of the Swans*, *Perekop*, and fragments of one not yet finished: *Poem of the Tsar's Family*—writings so intimate that it would be fatal to know that they had been read by enemies' eyes, a tiny drop in the vast sea of her production. Everything else, everything, it can be said, was scattered throughout the homes of friends, or people who were friends and became enemies, or who refused her access for fear of implicating themselves. After returning from exile, Ariadna dug for clues about writings from Moscow, Berlin, Belgrade, Prague, Paris, and uncovered hard-to-find editions and texts published in magazines and newspapers that had not existed for decades, as well as those unpublished. Thanks to her daughter's methodical and selfless activity, the body of the work remained complete, except for a few minor pieces. Almost everything recovered has been published. Ariadna, before dying, placed in the custody of a Soviet Institute of Literature various folders that she deemed inconvenient to be made public before the year 2000. This legacy may provide immense surprises. It is possible that some enigmas will be cleared up.

The response to Tsvetaeva's work has taken on in the past two decades an epiphanic quality, an immense and unexpected revelation. During the years of War Communism, during the time of famine, chaos, uncertainty, alone in a chaotic Moscow, when Sergei Efron was away, a conscript in the Tsarist regular army and then the White Army of General Wrangel, little Ariadna was her mother's closest friend, her confidante. At times, Marina became a little girl, and her daughter transformed into a rare phenomenon that surprised everyone; she read what her mother read, spoke as she spoke, recited Rilke and Homer; Tsvetaeva's friends were left speechless in her presence. She was the first person to whom her mother read her poems, her prose, her letters to her family, colleagues, friends. And the little girl commented as if they were peers on the rhythm, or the effectiveness of this or that effect that could perfect her writing. A decade later, in Czechoslovakia, when Georgy was born, called Mur from birth in honor of Hoffmann's fictional cat, Ariadna was pushed aside and placed for a time in a boarding school for Russian children in the Czech countryside. Upon returning home, the child prodigy who handled rhetoric with unimaginable virtuosity had become a girl on the brink of adolescence, who had become almost normal. She grows distant from her mother, for whom Mur is everything, and increasingly closer to her father, that melancholy being, always in delicate health, tossed aside by everyone, powerless before life, whom she chose to view this way. Thereafter, she lived in his shadow, and adopted his ideas. For Efron, the years in the White Army were a nightmare; they left him traumatized. On his father's side, he was Jewish; his mother, an aristocrat, a runaway from a very young age, a militant in terrorist societies, spent various periods of time behind bars, and ended up committing suicide, just as her eldest son had, at the end of a trial in which she would surely have been convicted. Anti-Semitism was endemic in the reactionary sectors of the country; in Crimea, in Ukrainian Galicia, pogroms were the order of the day. Cutting off the beards of Jews, destroying their businesses, beating them were everyday occurrences, an amusing sport, regardless of whether the victims were old men, women, or children. If one died from the beating, it would not anger Our Lord; on the contrary, it might even mean an indulgence to forgive the batterer's sins. To be a part of and live for years among those people who hated someone like him as if it were totally natural, a Jew, sickly, a *literato*, not leaving sooner was one of the greatest mistakes of this story. Of course, there were many others.

For seven years it seems that they saw each other only once clandestinely, or he took advantage of some other way to give Marina news of his life and announce that once the Tsar's army was defeated he would join the White Army in the Crimea. Marina's extremely harried life in Moscow at this time is well known, recorded in magnificent autobiographical essays. She endured hunger and extreme poverty, although it seemed to go reasonably unnoticed because almost everyone lived in the same conditions. With the help of an acquaintance, after the death of her second child due to a lack of money, she obtained a credential necessary to receive a modest living allowance and food vouchers.

She wrote several books that helped affirm her literary presence. She had numerous affairs, hurried, intense, frenzied, and unhappy at the same time. She wrote a book with no hope of being published that she considered the best she had written to date: *The Demesne of the Swans*, civil and epic poetry, a salute to the best, the Whites, the warriors against the revolutionary hydra of a thousand heads, the knights of good among whom was her beloved Sergei. After having not seen him for so many years, she had transformed him into an epic figure—he was Siegfried, he was Parsifal—and very rarely the poor and sickly Sergei, that beautiful and docile creature whom she had married in her adolescence, whom she didn't even know was still alive, fighting against evil and for the sake of Russia or buried in the south in an unmarked grave. When they finally reunited in Berlin, she introduced him immediately to Andrei Bely, the great Russian Symbolist, anticipating that they would become good friends. Tsvetaeva wrote the scene: "I remember Bely's special, intensified attentiveness to him [Sergei Efron], attention directed to each word, attention for each word, that special avidity of the poet for the world of action, avidity with even a glimmer of envy… (Let us not forget, that all the poets of the world have loved military men.)"[6] For Efron, the opposite was true, nothing seemed more repellent to him than his recent military past; he could not forget the humiliations he had endured during those years, the cruelties with which he had lived. Marina found it difficult to understand, much less hear him say, that the political movement that was unfolding in Russia was very complex and very difficult to understand from Europe, which is why the educated Russians,

---

6   Translated by J. Marin King.

like they themselves and their friends, could not understand it; they were all educated as Europeans, she insisted. Russia is only half European; the other half of its spirit is Asian. When he arrived in Berlin, he read his wife's dithyrambic poems to the swans whose elegant plumage alone was enough to defeat the Bolsheviks. He told her that none of it made sense, either aesthetically or ethically. To publish that book would be a moral error. Her reputation would be tarnished. It would be an affront to the Jews murdered by the Cossacks, and to the Russian peasants dispossessed by the Whites, "it would be an affront to your intelligence and poetry," he said. "The best you can do," he insisted, "is destroy, burn those papers, and forget about them. They are not swans, Marina, they are vultures, believe me." Marina was very distressed; she stopped defending her work in public because Sergei demanded it. She loved his military tone, it was an order; but she did not destroy the poems.

During his years of absence, she had invented a husband. Afterwards, she did not know how to take him. Her love for him was not constant—it waxed and waned. It would always be this way. In 1915, she wrote to her sister-in-law: "I love Seriozha for life, he is my very own and I will never leave him for anyone. I write him at least every other day, he knows all about my life, though I try to write less about what is most sad [the death of Irina, their second daughter]. There is a burden in my heart always. I go to sleep with it and I wake up with it."[7]

And yet, during those very days she was carrying on a tumultuous affair and for all to see, with a second-rate poet named Sophia Parnok.

---

7   Translated by Simon Karlinksy.

The reunion in Berlin was difficult. Time had changed them. They had become different people and continued to be until the end. Sergei discovered that during the short time that Marina spent in Germany waiting for him, she had had a romantic relationship with someone else. He confided it in a letter to a mutual friend, the poet Voloshin, in whose house in Yalta the couple had met. In the letter, he said he had discovered that Marina had a lover; to be offended by it made no sense, seven years had passed without seeing each other, and in all that time she had been free as they had agreed when they married. He was writing to him about something more serious, to announce that he had thought about dissolving their marriage, that he had decided to leave Marina. Her stupid affairs made him ill, and the last lover, about whom she claimed to be more passionate than ever, was a despicable man, a second-rate Casanova; that his youthful passion for her had disappeared, that he had planned to leave her, but on later reflection decided to sacrifice himself, because Marina was weak and would not survive such a bad experience without his help. At the same time, Marina wrote to a friend that living with Sergei was impossible, that "his very presence gnawed at her soul." But she knew that without her he would not be able to survive, "after all, I came abroad to join Sergei. Without me he would perish—from the simple inability to manage his life."[8] They both convinced themselves that they had each sacrificed for the other to save their marriage. For Marina the crisis was intense, serious, it left her shattered in body and spirit, but as everyone knew, each of these disasters invariably increased her creative powers.

---

8   Also translated by Karlinsky.

Thereafter, the marriage took on another character. Efron lost face with his friends in Prague; his closeness to Marina's lover turned out to be extremely awkward for him, they had been friends since youth, they were both officers in the White Army, and studied together in Prague in the Faculty of Philology. From then on, the intimacy between father and daughter begins. A tacit pact of solidarity for life.

It is somewhat paradoxical that, once they all disappeared, and in the atrocious way in which they met their end, Marina Tsvetaeva's literary legacy continues to endure thanks to the daughter who was distant to her in the last fifteen years of her life, and that she put so much of the energy she had left after having suffered fifteen years in prison, to organize her file and collect and classify the unpublished texts and correspondence. Hers was not a vicarious life, but rather one of triumph. In her last twenty years, Ariadna was Marina's mother, her guide, the master of her destiny. Without her, we would not be able to read her.

Here I am again in Leningrad. Contrary to all expectations the weather is gorgeous, perfectly bright and almost warm. They booked me into the Evropeiskaya, the imperial hotel where I stayed seven or eight years ago, to attend the opening of the Orozco exhibition at the Hermitage. Mid-morning, I paid a courtesy visit to the city's Writers' Union, a beautiful palace with Rococo interiors that clash with the Soviet office furniture and especially with the functions of that graveyard. At no time was I able to broach any of the current topics. I'm wondering if Moscow reported how badly I behaved there and has given instructions to keep me quiet during my meeting with the writers. The writers who welcomed me talked only about literature (so to speak) and only on the importance of landscape in Russian narrative. They spoke and gesticulated with exuberance; as soon as one was about to finish his monologue, another would take his place—a game of questions and answers. Someone asked a rhetorical and contrived question like: Is Soviet Russian literature not, perhaps, that which has most exalted nature, from the revolution to the present day?— while the one facing me answered: But, certainly, of course, the forest, the river, and the sea are themes that we cultivate most, also the desert, the steppe, the tundra, lakes so big they look like oceans, we have it all and of it all we sing. The only thing missing were the balalaikas so they could sing in honor of each of these formations of the earth's crust and also, in passing, the wildlife and minerals; in the meantime we drank coffee, ate cookies, desserts; and when the dishes were empty, they stood up, thanked me for the visit, accompanied me to the entrance, and before I realized it, I was already on the street. In the afternoon, a work of contemporary Russian theater about family problems, the lack of communication between generations; it bored me so much that I took advantage of the intermission to sneak out. I ran out into the street and walked. I walked for hours and hours. What splendor! Truly! There is nothing as splendid, intense, and tragic as this city! What melancholy! I spent part of the walk chatting with an Uzbek journalist, whom I met in a second-hand bookshop on Gorky Street. We spoke, as far as my Russian allowed, about literature and cities. He was amazed that I knew his country: Tashkent, Samarkand, Bukhara. He didn't want to talk about his country's current political or social affairs either, and he avoided the few questions I ventured, as if he had no interest in what was happening at the time, which means he wasn't pleased with the current moves, or that he was overly cautious and, because he did not know me from Adam, it was better to remain silent to avoid problems at work, for example. I got to my room half an hour ago. I read a few pages of *The White Ship*, by Chingiz Aitmatov, and I underlined these lines: "It is said, and not in vain, that people do not forgive the man who is unable to demand respect. He did not know how... He was softhearted, and that thankless human quality was apparent at first glance."[9] Later I pulled out another quote from one of Canetti's diaries from an Italian magazine, which he wrote the day he turned fifty-five: "Learn to speak again at fifty-five, not a new language but speech itself. Discard all my prejudices, even if nothing else is left. Reread the great books whether I've actually read them before or not. Listen to people without lecturing them, especially those who have nothing to teach me. Stop validating fear as a means of fulfillment. Struggle against death without constantly pronouncing its name. In short, courage and justice."[10] I, who transcribes those thoughts, will in three years turn fifty-five, Canetti's age when he wrote those words…Learn language, learn to speak, and learn that one does not have to want to be respected…that life is something much more mysterious and simpler…that should be the journey. I will make every effort, with courage and justice, as much as I can. ¡Ojalá! I hope!

---

9   Translated by Mirra Ginsburg.

10   Translated by John Hargraves.

I woke up in a mood from hell. I still don't know if I'll go to Georgia, and if so, when and for how many days. I took a long walk through parts of old Leningrad. I realize that I know nothing about the city, or very little. The same happens when I return to Rome, where I lived a few months in my youth, to Venice, where I have been several times, and Prague, where I have resided for three years. I get excited when I arrive, and I am stunned at the splendor of those dazzling cities; I realize that I continue to be in love with them, but I find that I am still a long way away from knowing them, that I have not managed to cross the threshold, that I'm just beginning to scratch their surface, and sometimes not even that. I have an urgent need to reread Andrei Bely's *Petersburg*, perhaps the most important Russian novel of the century. Mann read it in his youth and that reading marked him forever. At that time he detested that the novel had not remained in Stendhal, Tolstoy, or Fontane. They were extraordinary, no one could doubt it, but he found in Bely an almost secret parodic form. The culminating scenes, the violent climaxes that abound in the story are bathed in a gentle sarcasm that almost nobody noticed at the time. He did, and he began to study the construction of situations that could combine pathos with caricature. An example can be seen in the tuberculosis spots on the lungs of Mme Chauchat seen in an X-ray by Hans Castorp and the verbal spasm, the exquisite rhetoric with which this young man makes us aware of his romantic passion by way of these spots. I would like to read Bely's other novels: *The Silver Dove*, his most experimental, an intrauterine monologue that struggles, through babbling, to reach some meaning, and moreover, to soak in the amazing literature of early twentieth century at the end of teens and twenties: Akhmatova, Rozanov, Kuzmin, Tsvetaeva, Mandelstam, Tynyanov, Pasternak, Platonov, and Khlebnikov—for some the latter is the most radical poet of form at the time. Both Ripellino and Shklovsky, who have studied him thoroughly, agree that he is the true transformer of Russian lyrical poetry, who frees it from symbolism and directs it toward the avant-garde, toward futurism in particular. In the afternoon, a pleasant outing to the house-museum of Repin, a painter from the end of the nine-teenth century; we are indebted to him for the faces known to us of the great figures of the nineteenth century: Tolstoy, Turgenev, the whole lot. The house is on the Karelian peninsula, not far from the border with Finland. I grew bored during the outing; I continued to rehash my regret for having alienated the Russians. Only one of my books does not cause me to blush, *Vals de Mefisto* [Mephisto's Waltz], perhaps because when I wrote it, during the long period I lived in Moscow, I had immersed myself full-time in those waters. And in the evening a perfect *Eugene Onegin* at the Maly Theater. The only works of Tchaikovsky that really interest me are his operas. Orchestra, voices, musical and stage direction, set design, everything was remarkable in that masterful opera. I left the theater thoroughly refreshed. Happy to discover that my love of opera has not become extinct, as I sometimes feared. What bombs I've had to endure in Mexico in recent years! I remember an *I puritani* by Bellini[11] that Luz del Amo took me to see some time ago at Bellas Artes to calm my nerves the night before my standardization exam in the Foreign Service, and I still get shudders remembering that performance. But one can also experience these disappointments in Prague: whether out of apathy, desolation, or laziness, opera has become tedious, except when a major international figure arrives, then the singers and the orchestra give it everything they can, and the improvement is obvious. During intermission, I heard both Russian and Finnish. I have a nagging desire to go out onto the street. But I restrain myself. I think about cities: Prague, Moscow, and Leningrad. Prague is one of the most beautiful cities in the world, as everyone knows, and also the most hermetic. But the hopelessness of its inhabitants creates a gloom that permeates everything and penetrates to the marrow. Moscow has wonders: the churches of the Kremlin, St. Basil's, old neighborhoods—but also large areas of horrendous architecture. The monumental towers constructed during Stalinism are truly frightening, the megalomania of cement and reinforced concrete. An architecture that evinces a complete disregard for dreams, for any sense of play. But the city is alive, its breath can be felt everywhere. At the very moment I write this, there are probably thousands of Muscovites in open conflict, arguing,

---

11   Pitol mistakenly attributes the opera to Donizetti in the Spanish text. —*Trans.*

showing solidarity for each other, wanting to kill each other. Leningrad, the city of Peter, is also wonderful, and much more, is it not? But during these two days I have not felt its pulse. Sure, I have friends there, or acquaintances, and none here, and that makes a major difference. But there, even if someone brings up a political topic, even strangers say what they think. They are either followers or enemies of something. When I have tried here to cautiously talk about what is happening in the country, I encounter evasion, silence, polite changes of subject…

25 MAY

I left Prague with a bit of a cold. When I wake up, the first thing I do is take an analgesic and repeat the dose throughout the day, depending on how I feel. Last night and this morning I caught a cold and I realized that rhinitis has gotten the better of me. What spasms! My nostrils are stopped up, making it difficult to breathe, a howl-inducing migraine. I ate breakfast and walked to the Hermitage. I went up to the Picasso and Matisse rooms, to start the tour from there. These works were acquired before the revolution to dress the walls of the palace salons built by industrialists and financiers of the time; the newly fledged, extremely rich, educated and with very broad interests, unprejudiced toward the avant-garde, possibly advised by professors of aesthetics, connoisseurs of contemporary trends. And they accepted them effortlessly, indeed, happily. *Dance* and *Music* are housed here, immense in size; each of these great paintings could cover the largest wall of a salon. All of the other paintings, dozens, are also of high quality. They horrified the French, and in general the European, bourgeoisie, produced by wild beasts for the amusement of wild beasts. In the center of an exhibition hall stood a magnificent bronze by Donatello.

This space was responsible for housing a sample of the new generation: Matisse, Bonnard, the pointillists. People were crossing the room quickly, their eyes half-closed to keep their gaze from pausing on such monstrosities. A critic who walked through the hall wrote an article for a major newspaper with the headline: "Donatello among the wild beasts," and the young painters were happy and took the name: Wild Beasts (*fauves*). The Russian aristocracy loathed these objects viscerally, even more than the French bourgeoisie. It was the grandchildren and great-grandchildren of their former serfs, the new wealthy class, who felt comfortable surrounded by the form and color of beasts in their surroundings, which explains why many of the best Picassos and Matisses are still in Moscow and St. Petersburg. They were an integral part of the art nouveau villas of Russian magnates. I stayed a good while in these rooms and then meandered slowly past the others, almost without seeing the paintings due to a new migraine attack. I finally found Zurbarán's *Childhood of the Virgin*, which I knew only by photograph, but which in my previous visits was always traveling, and there I was revived…At lunchtime, I told a female employee of the Writers' Union, who accompanied me at meals and to shows, about my previous visit to the museum, framed by privileged conditions: it must have been in 1980 or 1981. A delegation from Mexico had arrived in Leningrad: Juan José Bremer, Rafael Tovar, Carmen Beatriz López Portillo, and Fernando Gamboa, and from Moscow, Ambassador Rogelio Martínez Aguilar, Elzvieta, his wife, and some officials from our diplomatic mission, including myself, to inaugurate a monumental exhibition of Orozco the following day. The director of the Hermitage had prepared a tour of some of the museum's rooms. It was Monday, the day when museums close their doors to the public. Our entourage, a dozen people, resembled a tiny group of lost caterpillars in its majestic halls. We toured immense corridors, went up and down imperial staircases. Without the public, the building was once again the Winter Palace, the residence of the Tsars; its dimensions multiplied and escaped to infinity. One could hardly benefit from those conditions to enjoy what awaited: *The Venus Tauride*, the extensive collection of primitive and Renaissance Italians, the Cranaches, the vast Rembrandt room, the Spaniards, the Impressionists, until finally arriving at Matisse and Picasso on the top floor. What delighted me most, of this superb visual feast, was after having reviewed for several hours the entire history of Western art, upon arriving to the main floor, where Gamboa and his team were putting the final touches to the Mexican exhibition, the works of Orozco did not stand out from the tradition of great painting but rather continued it. The effect was splendid and revealing. Our great artist belonged, just as Matisse and Picasso, although with a distinct poetics, to the great artistic legacy of the twentieth century. In the afternoon, a lightning visit to the home of Alexander Blok, which has just become a museum. Very moving, but I didn't have anyone to talk about Blok with—about his time, about poetry in general, the Scythians, whom Blok revered, those kinds of things. I don't know anyone in Leningrad, and despite the city's undeniable beauty, its more extensive contact with foreign tourists and their customs (in restaurants, at the opera, in museums, in antique shops and bookstores, one hears almost as much Finnish as Russian and, also, a great deal of Swedish and German), its rich cultural traditions,

its sumptuous past, its sophistication, it also gives off a sudden
aroma of pretentiousness and provincialism that is not perceived
in the least in barbaric Moscow, whose vitality has been irresist-
ible, if one accepts the testimony of two centuries of chronicles
and novels. Perhaps the Second World War brought an end to the
intellectual heyday of this imperial capital. A large number of its
writers, artists, scientists, died during the siege or were evacuated
to safer places, and when peace came they didn't return. It was
a broken city. Many settled in Moscow, where surely there must
have been better conditions: publishing houses, universities and
schools, libraries, research centers, a literary press, the movie studios. For this remarkable city to be truly perfect—perfect for me,
that is—it would require the existence, inserted in the folds and
crevices of its oldest neighborhoods, of a Kitay-gorod, that invisible
Asian city that Boris Pilnyak yearned for, which according to him
is hidden inside all authentically Russian cities, where countless
eyes, mere horizontal slits drawn on an inscrutable facial surface,
contemplate everything, study it, interpret it, and where in the
darkness of the seedier areas marinates an indescribable mixture of
fierce emotions, atavistic terrors, unfathomable mysteries, adven-
tures and exorbitant mountains of dust, layers of innumerable coats
of paint embedded on the old walls; in short, to hear the echo of
the Scythians invoked by Blok, a Mongolian appetite to stain the
European city…In the afternoon, a brief but torrential rain. When
the sky cleared, and the lead weight on the atmospheric pressure
vanished, my nose began to open up and my migraine vanished
immediately. I went to the theater to see Gogol's *The Wedding*.
A less-than discrete performance, an excessively convoluted stage

direction, with all the refined, useless, and unbearable affectations to which Stanislavsky has been reduced in the hands of certain pretentious directors. It is impossible to compare this *Wedding* with the intelligent production of *The Inspector* I saw a few days ago in Moscow! We left the theater under a heavy rain. I'll try to read some of Mandelstam's *Journey to Armenia*, which I began after lunch. I've had too much bread, creams, pastries, blinis, and caviar. My clothes feel tight. Starting tomorrow, I'll make the necessary adjustments…Later, I lost the desire to read, not even Mandelstam. At midnight, I couldn't resist the temptation and went out to wander beneath an entirely white sky. I walked the length of Nevsky Prospect from the railway station to the Hermitage; the grand avenue is a recurring scene in Russian literature, from Pushkin to the present. I am and am not in Leningrad. Am I? Of course I am! It's as if I never left. What a lie! My heart is somewhere else.

GOLDFISH

I was in my second year of secondary school. My grandmother had given me a small rigid leather attaché to hold my books, notebooks, and other school supplies, in the hope that I would stop losing them all the time. We had a subscription to a medical journal with excellent illustrations from which you could detach reproductions of masterpieces of art. I used to cut out these pages and keep them in a box of personal treasures.

One day, when I opened the magazine, I was stunned. I had never seen anything as dazzling as that colorful page. A picture bathed in light, lit from above, but also from inside the canvas. Goldfish were swimming in a fishbowl, their reflection rocking on the surface of the water. It was the absolute triumph of color. The pail containing the fish was part of the vertical axis of the painting and rested on a round table held up by a single foot. It was, of course, in the center. The rest of the canvas was a forest of beautiful leaves and flowers; they were in the foreground, in the background, they could be seen through the glass container, aroused, clustered, together, luminous, perfect. If I had lived in Antarctica, or in the heart of Sonora, or the

Sahara, where nobody ever saw flowers or fish or water, I could understand how this flowery precipitation could drive me mad. But I lived in Córdoba, next-door to Fortín de las Flores, in the midst of succulent gardens, and yet it seemed like a miracle to me. I glued the page to the hard inner part of my case, where some classmates placed photos of Lucha Reyes, Toña la Negra—the great voices of the time—or boxers, movie scenes, dogs, Virgins and Saints, or snazzy models of airplanes or automobiles; others, nothing. I lived with my goldfish and their fascinating surroundings for three years. It was my best amulet—a sign, a promise. Later I saw reproductions of other works by its author, but not that one. At the Museum of Modern Art in New York I stopped in amazement in front of his formidable oils.

Years later, as I entered a room in the Pushkin Museum in Moscow, which houses some of Matisse's most extraordinary oils, I suddenly came across the original of my goldfish. It was more than an aesthetic experience—it was a mystical trance, an instant reassessment of the world, of the continuity of time.

Nowhere have I dreamt so much as in Russia. My notes from my time as cultural attaché are proof of it. I would wake up at night and write down the outline of a dream, I would climb into a car and although the ride would last only ten minutes, I would dream something. I dreamt during the siesta, in a boring meeting, at a movie, anywhere. Dreams appeared in bulk. The height of extravagance. *Mephisto's Waltz*, née *Bukhara Nocturne*, emerged from those dreams. And on this trip, the same is happening. On the plane, coming from Prague I dreamt I ran into a classmate from the Faculty of Law, a dead man pretending to be alive, which I didn't find the least bit amusing, and last night I had another dream that was interrupted when I went to the bathroom, and which I summarized as I went back to bed in four or five lines. When I woke the next morning I read what I had written and thought it was very funny. I don't know why. It could have been, I think, if in the dream I'd been a mere witness to what happened and not a protagonist. I'll try to describe it sparingly, removing the frills that have come to plague my work in recent years. I'm in Moscow, eating breakfast in the restaurant of the National. I recognize three or four famous international figures in the middle of a large group of writers. Suddenly I see the writer Catalina D'Erzell, a Mexican playwright, and I turn to greet her. I never met her when she was alive, I had perhaps seen a photo of her in a newspaper, but I don't remember what she looks like at all. She had a modicum of fame in the forties and perhaps early fifties. I never saw her plays, nor have I read them. They were lachrymose and prim melodramas, of which the titles are proof: *What Only a Man Can Suffer*, *The Sin of Women*, *Those Men!* In the dream, I went to say hello and she told me that a conference on Slavic literature was beginning that day, that we, the only Mexicans—what an honor, what a tribute!— would open the first session, and she was a little nervous because she had not seen me in a few days. She would not have been able to translate alone into body language the Chekhov story we had chosen. Not even if they gave her an award, not even if they threatened to lock her up for life in a Siberian dungeon would she do it alone. Whom would she have as a partner? Who would know how to express all the registers of *The Murder*? She doubted that other than us anyone was competent enough. On the bus, Señora D'Erzell explained to me that she had for months prepared ways to interpret in extremely tense forms of body language the genius of Anton Pavlovich Chekhov. *The Murder* is one of the most difficult novellas to interpret. "There is a lot of philosophy, I can tell you, in this battle between two relatives who believe in God, one of them is convinced that Our Lord was born and died to teach men to live with dignity and happiness, while the other, who spends all his time in religious ceremonies, all the while stealing from his fellow parishioners using all kinds of tricks, believes that Christ is the equivalent of a punishment. That is my reading, full of philosophy as you can see. It's a pity that you didn't go to the university auditorium yesterday. I did the finale alone, they asked me, I couldn't escape the commitment and, since you were not there, what was I to do. I expressed with my whole body the Christian revelation, the true epiphany, the stern brother who resorts to crime finds himself in a sinister prison, where he is stripped of everything, they beat him, insult him, and there, at last, he has begun to love God, to understand that He wishes us to love each other, to help each other, which also coincides with my philosophy. I don't know what yours is, but whatever it is, I beg you, during the *largo desolato* at the end, which is so difficult, please hold me firmly, one long step, three tiny ones, one long and three short, do you understand?" I didn't understand anything, not a word. What incredibly silly stunt were we about to pull in front of the public?…What a bunch of nonsense?…Suddenly we were on center stage. The music began to play, it was "Falling in Love Again," Marlene Dietrich's signature song. My compatriot, dressed entirely in black, with a corset that gave her the body of a dolphin in vertical jump, but a body nonetheless, rolled several times across the stage, at times with the slow ferociousness of a jaguar, others with the tenderness that the spectator always associates with the cooing of doves. I was almost hidden on one side of the stage, at times she approached me, bowed, extended her arm, pointed at me and then turned to the audience with a sweeping gesture that enveloped me and the audience. Suddenly, from the loudspeakers came a velvety but firm voice, serious, even severe one might think, that introduced us as the two greatest experts of Russian literature, especially Chekhov, not only in Mexico but throughout the Americas. The praise showered on the lady was excessive, a little extravagant, I would say, for example, they announced her as "the internationally-recognized supreme empress of Chekhov, heroic woman who has danced on Parnassus, but also splashed pitifully through the mud, a firefly and tarantula, a wholly dialectical being, from head to toe." I then discovered that we were not in a university auditorium, but in a circus, and that the audience was not made up of academics or intellectuals but rather what one finds in circuses: families, children, noise, happiness, and among the throng of everyday people one could see the faces of the international dignitaries attending the Conference. A woman in a military uniform hugged my partner's waist, took her by the arm to greet the public while at the same time demanding a warm applause, a cosmic applause to comfort the heart of the Mexican woman who had suffered so much and had stumbled so many times in life. She said it just like that. I, on the other hand, was nobody—a shadow, a zero to the left. Anyone who has suffered a spectacular automobile accident will be able to understand me: everything happens at once, everything is simultaneous, a bit like in *The Aleph*, one loses the ability to know for sure what came first and what next. The visions in the dream changed constantly, became interwoven with others, they transformed into a permanent metamorphosis. I will try to make a semblance of their order, a story in a more or less successive form, in spite of the endless fits and starts, the vocation for chaos privileged by dreams. A master of ceremonies announced in a divine voice the first act of the Conference: the body reading of Anton Chekhov's amazing and enigmatic gem: *The Murder*, performed by a famous Russian actress (not only famous but the most famous, my compatriot told me in a whisper), whose name was not mentioned, which I found strange, interpreted by the equally eminent bodybuilder Catalina D'Erzell and her assistant, also Mexican. D'Erzell in the meantime ordered me to "take a deep breath, relax, believe in God above all things, nimble feet, cool head, everything in its place," while two long rows of men on the right, and women on the left, climbed to the stage. "A chorus of basses and altos, baritones and mezzos, tenors and sopranos!" the speaker announced. "Voices of cannon and crinoline, as it should be!" my compatriot whispered in the voice of a little bird. A stately woman, dignified and beautiful, ascended to the rostrum and sat on a throne. Ray beams bathed us in light. The ceremony began. The actress began reading Chekhov's tale in an absolutely wonderful, lilting, superhuman voice; minutes later, the chorus began to repeat her words melodiously. The prose became music; the actress stopped talking, she sang the text and the choir sang with her, with spirit and splendor. At times the noise was deafening, enough to drive anyone mad, except, apparently, the attendees of the Conference of Slavic Literatures, who were fascinated. Who knows where the other smaller orchestra of balalaikas came from, that surrounded us during the body interpretation and followed our every step, faithful to the end! My compatriot commanded: "It's your turn, cannon," so I went: she made me do jumps of every caliber, squat on the floor, lift one leg, then the other, fall dead and rise again, run with my partner around the stage, lift her, throw her it into the air above my head, then stop her fall mere inches from the floor, then force her to maintain an upright position with her head down and feet up. Our greatest triumph was a series of turns we did on stage at a hair-raising speed, but also with absolute precision because had I released her, she would have crashed into the audience, and perhaps she and some spectators would have gone on to a better world, but our ability was extraordinary and there was not even the slightest incident. There were moments of dancing on point and others in which we jumped gaily and closed like accordions as we fell on the floor, only to propel ourselves immediately into the air by way of springs. We achieved ecstasy, delirium, another sky whose existence we never suspected, like in African ritual dances, at least I did. I was Nijinsky for a few moments, I was Nureyev, I swear, and she, no less than Terpsichore. The end of Chekhov's story was one of the most beautiful that one could ever imagine. The austere Christian, the repressor, has murdered his cousin, and is sentenced to life in prison in Siberia. There, amid terrible punishments, he rejects what he has been and finds true faith in God, a simple faith like that of his cousin whom he had so hated, and that gives him hope to truly live, to save someone from perdition, to redeem himself. Then the great climax: she could be heard moaning suddenly, as if she no could no longer continue, as if she were about to surrender, only to demand tremulously greater speed from me, more rhythm, more muscle. Suddenly everything stopped, the musicians disappeared with their balalaikas, silent and downcast they descended the stairs, and the choruses of basses and altos, baritones and mezzos, tenors and sopranos, light and absolute, and even the masterful actress whose name we never knew, who had read Chekhov's story.

Without saying a word we fell like whipped dogs. We passed around towels soaked in vinegar for our faces; fans began to approach us. The crowd, crazed with enthusiasm, surrounded D'Erzell, but nobody noticed me. I managed to sneak off the stage and wander through a mysterious maze of corridors and stairways, a scene similar to Piranesi's prisons, which slowly became a rickety passageway, and then an anodyne, ugly, gray street. An instant later, I was walking through an unfamiliar neighborhood. Some young people stopped next to me, looked at me, and one of them shouted rudely: "Wash your face, you clown son-of-a-bitch, or I'll wash it with bleach." A girl with beautiful eyes, the rest of her face covered by the collar of her coat, put a mirror in front of my face, and I almost threw up. The face I saw, rotten, decomposed, was telling me that I only had a few hours to live. What I can't understand is why, then, I woke up so happy and wrote so happily during the early morning hours the first draft of the dream. Why then hours later, wide-awake, did I think that I had a funny dream, which now, as I transcribe it, causes me unbearable anguish?

27 MAY

Yesterday I was on edge because of the dream in which I was dancing maniacally with Señora D'Erzell, whom I've never even met. During the day I remembered dancing scenes that made me laugh out loud, but at night as I was writing it down I detected a connection with some very old dreams, an absurd flowering of remorse back in my thirties, when I led a life disposed to revelry, carousing, a so-called wanton's life, and arrived home at dawn only to fall asleep without fail and dream that I had lost my way, that if I didn't straighten up I'd be a failure, and in those early-morning dreams I was often demeaned in the eyes of my teachers and especially my comrades of letters, my disciplined and efficient contemporaries, low blows that fortunately disappeared in an instant when I woke up at noon, freeing me to act however I wanted. Once I reviewed the dream, I found that its meaning was just the opposite of those juvenile moralizing dreams; it was instead a way to laugh at myself, to dive head first into the carnival, to live my destiny as the Ugly King and receive that well-deserved beating with which that king's tale ends. The height of carnival. But I'm furious because I've had problems with representatives of the Writers' Union who apparently do not want to allow me to go to Georgia, and especially because of a terrible incident, a comedy of errors that caused me to feel extreme panic and triggered a nightmare worse than any I can remember. I'll begin: at breakfast time a very unctuous and talkative employee of the Writers' Union arrived, asking if everything was going well in the city, that they, the Association and its leaders, were happy about my visit, and they wanted to invite me to participate day-after-tomorrow with other foreign experts in a major symposium in the city of Tula on Turgenev's work, that they had already talked about it with my embassy and that the cultural attaché had thought it a perfect idea. I told him bluntly that the embassy had no right to decide for me; my visit was not official; I insisted that I had taken this trip in response to an invitation from Georgian writers and therefore did not understand why other activities were being proposed for me. The messenger seemed to agree with everything, but said that an ambassador from one country never ceases to have an official connotation in another country, and that in the USSR all associations of writers, painters, pilots, doctors—of any profession—were autonomous organizations, yes, but official nonetheless. It was a dialogue of the deaf; I kept insisting: why this stubbornness to keep me from traveling to Georgia? He should tell his superiors that I would return to Prague this afternoon, that I would also communicate with my embassy to make them aware of the circumstances in which this visit was unfolding. He said he would, but for the moment, since a tour that morning was planned to a number of Pushkin-related sites in the city and its surroundings, he was sure that I would find a visit to the town of Pushkin fascinating.

I refused, I told him that I'd rather rest and get everything ready for the trip and to please advise me when the plane to Prague was leaving. The employee did not bat an eyelid, he drank the last sips of his coffee, looked around, then stared at the book on the table, *Jen Sheng*, by Mikhail Prishvin, in Italian translation, and next to the book a notecard where I had just made some notes. I had brought the book to study the close relationship that Russian literature maintains with nature that has always impressed me. On the notecard I had written: "Yes, in my hermitage I convinced myself, once and for all, that scented soaps and clothes brushes represent only a small part of civilization, that the essence of civilization resides above all in the creative force of understanding oneself, and of forming a bond between men…" He pointed to the book. He wanted to continue talking, but apparently wasn't sure how, and I wasn't going to help him; he was busy eating cheese and bread…Finally, he said that he had studied Italian as a second language in university, that he liked it a lot, but that it was well below his knowledge of Spanish. He looked for ways to convince me to go to the Turgenev celebration but was unable to find one. I got up from the table and told him coldly to call me as soon as he arranged my departure from Leningrad. After returning to my room I was overcome with a terrific flash of rage. I called the embassy in Moscow and Luz del Amo in Mexico. I lay down on the bed. I was exhausted. I tried to sleep a bit longer and forget the insignificant gray man who had visited me to divert me from Georgia. I fell asleep and before doing so completely I felt a sealike calm in anticipation of Catalina D'Erzell's inviting me to dance with her again, but not *The Murder*, instead a longer piece, with more dazzling effects that would allow me to really shine in front of the distinguished audience, like *The Cherry Orchard*, for example. I woke up an hour later, without remembering any dream, but in a much better mood. Absolutely determined to not give in. I left the hotel, went to the used bookstore on Nevsky Prospect, about two or three blocks from the hotel. When I arrived at the bookstore I had second thoughts. What if at that very moment the writers were calling me to tell me that everything was set to leave for the airport and fly to Tbilisi or Prague, which was all the same to me anyway? And later they would tell me that they had looked for me, that they had everything arranged and since they didn't find me in my room as we had agreed, they had to cancel the flight, I would have to accompany them to Tula and improvise a talk on the author of *Fathers and Sons*. My concern forced me to make a doctor's visit, without pausing to rummage through the shelves as long as I had wanted. I found a copy of Karlinsky's book on Gogol's dark sexuality that I had been searching for over a period several years; an anthology of stories by Boris Pilnyak, which included an original, splendid, and virulent story that had been on my mind since my arrival in the city: "His Majesty Kneeb Piter Komondor," a quasi-demented diatribe in its stubbornness against the Westernization imposed by Peter the Great in Russia; and in the English section, *Mr. Byculla*, a detective novel by Eric Linklater, which I read as a teenager in *The Seventh Circle* by Borges and Bioy Casares, that fascinated me at the time—a very complicated story of a criminal religious sect whose plots unfolds throughout the centuries. Twice I had bought the original English edition, only to lose it almost immediately both times.

Today's, the third, was the quickest. Upon arriving to the hotel room, I found only the books by Pilnyak and Karlinsky in the bag. I could not have left *Mr. Byculla* at the bookstore because I was perusing it with delight on the street. I went down to the café, pointed to the table where I was sitting, and they responded that no waiter had picked up a book. "As you can see," the employee said, "we've had a lot of people this morning, someone might have taken it;" I then asked at reception, where I had stopped for a moment to ask if anyone had phoned me, and no, no one had, nor had anyone left anything. I went up to my room, asked for my key from the gruff *matryoshka* who was guarding the floor—one of those robust and gritty women clad in a horrendous paramilitary uniform responsible for the supervision and control of guests. I asked her if I had left a book there when I asked for the key five minutes earlier. Not a single facial feature changed, only her hard eyes opened until becoming round like those of a sinister doll, she opened the desk drawer without taking her eyes off me and pulled out two Finnish pornographic magazines—one was obviously *Tom of Finland*, the magnificent line of the figures was unmistakable. On the cover two young policemen are entertaining themselves in horseplay; one is unbuttoning the pants of his partner's uniform with one hand while removing from his own fly with the other a tool capable of destroying an elephant's vagina. The two cops' eyes are shining as they lick their lips with pleasure. The face of that monument to the police force before me turned a shade of purple, like a huge dark tomato, as she looked at the cover, and in a faint but sharp voice that did not at all match the stature and strength of her body—instead of the booming deep bass voice one would expect—she said that the police were to be respected, and anyone who spreads subversive propaganda in the Soviet Union, especially when it intends to degrade the courageous men and women who make up the security of the State, has to pay the appropriate penalty for his criminal effrontery. She concluded: "So were you the one who left them in the room? And you still have the nerve to claim them! Give me your key, give me the key to your room, if you resist you will regret it. Give it to me." She addressed me with *ty*, the Russian pronoun that denotes familiarity or, in this case, impertinence, with a delicate but firm voice and soldierly expression. "Either you give it to me willingly, or I'll break your neck." She stood up and held out her hand. To say I was terrified would be an understatement. I realized that they had set a cruel trap for me. The next day my picture would be splashed across the newspapers enveloped in a cloud of scandal; I would be expelled from the country amid terrible humiliation. All this for wanting to go to Georgia and not to the celebrations for Turgenev? Or for having behaved rudely the day the president of the Writers' Union invited me to lunch? I gave her the key. The monster saw the number, showed a look of surprise, changed her tone, and asked my name, which I gave to her. She fell into her chair with an expression of bewilderment. She asked me with extreme courtesy for an identification other than my passport. Thank God she was no longer addressing me with *ty*. She covered the *Tom of Finland* magazines with a towel. She carefully studied my diplomatic card, and then said in a voice that had become a fearful trill: "Forgive me, citizen, there has been a mistake. You say that you came to pick up a book; but no one has given me a lost book, this is the time when all the tourists vacate their rooms and leave them in a mess—the beds, the furniture filled with books of anti-Soviet propaganda, yes, and in every language of the world." Just then, there appeared in the corridor an elderly couple, very elegant people, the woman wearing an extremely luxurious fur coat, with a carriage and gestures that were indisputably from *le grand monde*; he, a little weathered, was supporting himself on an orthopedic cane, and at his side a translator, or secretary, also very well dressed. They stopped at the table, with wide smiles, as if they were very satisfied with their stay, and spoke Finnish with their companion. He said something dry and authoritative to the woman, and she handed them the pornographic magazines. The interpreter spoke to her with a tone of implacable authority; when she meekly surrendered the publications, he smirked, patronizingly, almost with contempt, and she, the terrible guardian of order who had so frightened me, acted like a little girl, a reprimanded pupil, and raised her shoulders slightly, as if to apologize. And I didn't understand anything. Who were these elderly people? Why did they claim those magazines? What powers did they have? Mysteries of the great beyond. I remembered a novel by Highsmith, of whom I am quite fond lately: *A Dog's Ransom*, in which a young policeman is terrorized by a thug, a poor sinister devil, who accuses him, the policeman, once his crime is discovered, of demanding from him a percentage of everything he got in his acts of villainy. And I thought how vulnerable someone, anyone, can be when someone else makes an absurd accusation, spreads a slanderous lie, and maintains it without backing down. I lay on the bed again and took a sedative, all I wanted then was to return to Prague as quickly as possible, by train in the event there were no seats available on a plane, and I thought that dancing with Catalina D'Erzell had given me a frightful case of bad luck. Perhaps in life she had been jinxed, and during the course of that seemingly never-ending dance she had infused me with an essence that was pure *gettatura*—the evil eye. My bags were ready; I only needed to put away the medicines on the bedside table and some books. The interpreter called to tell me not to worry because the passage was booked; no, he did not know exactly what time we should leave the hotel, but I should please stay in the room, someone would go by the agency to collect the tickets and accompany me to the airport. Everything is set. What a relief! A ticket to where, I wondered after hanging up the phone. Would they be such sons-of-bitches as to return me to Prague? And why didn't they tell me exactly what time they would collect me? I could still see a thousand things in the city! Go to the Russian Museum, which was a step away, or closer, if only to see the façade; or the house where Anna Akhmatova lived and suffered, which to my knowledge is also very close, on the Fontanka. The last thing I read yesterday, for several hours, was the phantasmagoric *Evenings on a Farm near Dikanka* by Gogol: I read and reread that prodigious story titled "Ivan Fyodorovich Shponka and His Aunt," written after the author had just arrived to Petersburg from a village in Ukraine, a young man whom everyone mocked, and rightly so, because all he did was make foolish remarks and act a little off in the head, but with that story (and he would never know) he anticipated by at least a century and a half the best avant-garde literature. Every time I read it,

I become intoxicated with joy and amazement. It is unique in its genre. He wrote it during adolescence; the other stories that accompany it in the book are entirely foreign to it. It's a pity that I didn't read his *Evenings* until last night when I should have started them on my arrival in Leningrad. Doing so would have opened a parallel and antagonistic track to my travels. Witches, bloodshed everywhere, dementia, ghosts aplenty and of various kinds, the entire wicked lineage of evil. It would have been an effective anaphrodisiac to avoid falling to my knees in love with the city's extreme perfection. Just to think that these stories were conceived right there is enough. And not just in Leningrad should I have begun with Gogol, but from the very moment I boarded the plane that took me to Moscow…I would love to write a small book, five effigies against the backdrop of the imperial city: Pushkin, Gogol, Blok, Akhmatova, Bely—five personal hells. Or another, on diverse and very free topics, such as Mandelstam's casual notes on Armenia, which are digressions on a thousand different things that more often than not have nothing to do with Armenia, and remember the monumental figure of Marietta as she enters the auditorium of the International Library of Moscow, where I read my lecture, the corners of her lips, her sneer, the indifference she displayed to the world, and the pursuit of her husband's work, where, according to her, there were wonders unknown to anyone about feasts in Mexico, archaic rituals, among which the most exciting had to do with a child's defecation, an authentic rite of spring, a rebirth of the world.

FAMILY PORTRAIT II

I am a shadow of someone's shadow.

MARINA TSVETAEVA

I am impressed by the current veneration of Tsvetaeva by women. They are excited about her work, but, personally, I think what fascinates them most is her person. The Russian Irma Kudrova, however, in her preface to *A Captive Spirit,* surpasses all others:

> One of the brightest stars on the horizon of twentieth century Russian culture, Marina Tsvetaeva's name transcends literary fame alone. She was a unique personality, whose words embodied the rare richness of her soul, the immortality of her mind, and her uncompromising conscience. She fused the gift of poetry and passionate human essence into a tight union that infects a current tension into every line of her poetry.[12]

Very different from what other women of letters who dealt with her closely in life thought of her. Nadezhda Mandelstam

---

12   This and other translations from *Russian Life* do not give the name of the translator. —*Trans.*

met her in 1922, shortly before she emigrated from Moscow; she remembers her this way:

> My impression of Tsvetaeva was that she was absolutely natural and fantastically self-willed. I have a vivid recollection of her cropped hair, loose-limbed gait—like a boy's—and speech remarkably like her verse. Her willfulness was not just a matter of temperament but a way of life. She could never have reined herself in, as Akhmatova did. Reading Tsvetaeva's verse and letters nowadays I realize that what she always needed was to experience every emotion to the very utmost, seeking ecstasy not only in love, but also in abandonment, loneliness, and disaster. I can see there is a rare nobility of mind about this attitude, but I am disturbed by the accompanying indifference to people who at any given moment were not needed at her "feast of feelings."[13]

In Nina Berberova's memoirs, there are two testaments, one in Prague, from 1923, and another in Paris, from 1937:

> All that Tsvetaeva says interests me, there is a mixture of wisdom and whimsy in her speech; but there is almost always something alien to me, a sick strain that startles me, exhilarating, provocative, "clever", but somehow disturbing, without equilibrium, somehow dangerous for our further relations, as if we were now happy to fly

---

13   Translated by Max Hayward.

al00# SERGIO PITOL

over waves and thresholds, but the following moment we would bump into each other and get hurt. And I feel this. She obviously does not; she probably thinks in the future she can either become friendly with me or quarrel.[14]

And years later, shortly before leaving France:

I saw Marina Tsvetaeva for the last time in the autumn of 1938 at the funeral of Prince Volkonsky, at the moment his coffin was being out of the church (on the Rue François Gérard). She stood at the entrance, her eyes full of tears, aged, almost white, hands crossed on her bosom. This was soon after the murder of Ignace Reiss in which her husband, Efron, was implicated. She stood as if infected by a plague, no one approached her. Like everybody else I walked by her.[15]

They were writers of great moral strength, they were objective, not like the majority of Russians in Parisian circles, such as, for example, the impossible Zinaida Gippius, wife of Dmitri Merezhkovsky, who was considered a Russian queen exiled in France, and to whom a writer like Tsvetaeva, who admired Mayakovsky and Pasternak, could not be anything but scum.

An aficionado and advocate, a patient and loyal friend from her days in Prague until the end, Marc Slonim, a critic and historian of Russian literature, one of the first enthusiasts of her work in the

---

14   Translated by Philippe Radley.
15   Also translated by Radley.

West, who together with Svyatopolk-Mirsky proclaimed her one of the major poetic figures of her time, and not only in Russian terms, presents us the image of Marina, mocked by the mediocrity and pettiness of Russian exiles:

> In émigré Paris, Tsvetaeva obviously could not fit in at "court." Newspapers and journals tolerated her, in the best of times, but she often found the idea of collaborating with others offensive. She could never occupy a place in émigré "society" salons, political and literary circles where everyone knew each other…She remained forever the wild outsider, divorced from the group, and distinguished herself by her appearance, speech, outfits and mark of poverty…[16]

At nineteen, even before she published her first book of poetry and married Sergei, the seventeen-year old student of literature, Tsvetaeva, designed an exciting life project, free, without shackles, without limitations, similar to that of the Romantics. The contempt she had felt for Chekhov since her youth is due possibly to the fact that the universe he created exemplified the eclipse of the hero. The characters that inhabit Chekhov's stories and dramas, consumed by a febrile electricity, are antagonistic to romantic protagonists, the heroes of Pushkin or Lermontov. The Russian Romantics invented the writer as hero, a central figure, sacred, and when one says writer one should understand poet. Both Pushkin's life and death, like that of Lermontov, have a meaning identical

---

16   *Russian Life.*

to that of their characters: Onegin, Pechorin. Revolution is the quintessential romantic phenomenon. The indeterminate, the irrational, overlaps the determined. Passion is the point from which the revolution departs. The fluid, the ethereal, rebels against the inert stubbornness of paralyzed regimes, requiring a new form and a new discourse. We will have to destroy everything and discover everything. This is the conception of the nineteenth-century romantic poet as the only being who has a relationship with the universe, who listens for the unknown and from there utters the secret words. He alone has the right to speak with nature and the gods, because like them he knows all the secrets and possibilities of language. However, Marina detests revolution. Her romanticism requires power. Napoleon was one of her childhood heroes. From a young age, she knew what her place in poetry was. In language, she found the signs she was looking for. Her poetry is different from that of her contemporaries. She employs strong, clear nouns and names things accurately, but when her words approach each other they are transmuted into atmosphere, shadow, pain, despair. In her last decade, she wrote, above all, essays, and played freely with genre. Her essays are always a story and the kernel of a novel and a chronicle of time and a piece of autobiography.

She went to Paris in 1925, preceded by a mysterious halo. Rilke—no less!—had celebrated her. Critics surrendered to her, to her prestige, to the originality of her persona. Her public readings were attended by the most important Russian literary community in France for three or four months. But the exaltation of two Russian princes, both intellectuals, was enough to defeat her. Prince Dmitri Svyatopolk-Mirsky, a fan of her poetry from early on, who followed her from the beginning and saw her explode like a revelation, declared in Paris and in writing that she was the best Russian poet in Paris at the time; the other prince, the young Dmitri Shakhovskoy, who directed and financed a magazine of great beauty where every writer wanted to publish, invited her to collaborate on the third and final issue; The Prince wanted the issue to be exceptional because it not only marked the end of the magazine but also his stay in the world. He had already prepared his entrance into a silent order in a monastery on Mount Athos. The title of her article was "The Poet and Criticism;" therein Tsvetaeva made light of Paris's Russian critics, accusing them of ignorance and parochialism; they discredited modern poetry out of misinformation, due to their lack of culture. It was an arrogant and unforgiving essay, but it was sustained by literary truths and objective concepts. It marked the end of the cult of Tsvetaeva. She was never able to recover; but rather it was the first step of her descent into silence. Sergei Efron, who had never worked in his life, was invited by Prince Mirsky to collaborate with him and some other notable Russians to publish a literary magazine called *Milestones*, which would publish Russians from both outside and inside Russia, that is, those from within the inferno: Soviet Russia. Pasternak, Babel, Esenin, Tynyanov—a quite remarkable group in any world literary scene—were described in Paris by the most influential critic in exile, Peter Struve, as "mere carrion."

We know, and Tolstoy has reminded us with superb words, that each unhappy family is unhappy in a different way. The causes of unhappiness can be infinite. The effects, the gestures, the epidermis are observed from the outside; in day-to-day gossip we learn of countless cases of separation, amazing escapes, fairy-tale divorces, or other infinitely more sordid tales. We sometimes come out in favor of one or the other of the spouses. The violent husband, the frivolous wife, the excessive greed of one or both, the meddling of in-laws, relatives, friends, stupidity, jealousy, may all be elements of the plot. We know that and more, much more, but we never manage to measure the silent disagreement of the senses, nor the minutia hidden in the inner folds that are derivations of the physical, the battle of the sexes in all its aspects, and even if one or the other of the spouses confides in us, which is the worst that can happen to someone, and the abuses of friendship are horrifying, meticulously physiological, and make us believe that we know everything, it is in no way true. Everything they tell us, even when deformed by passion and anger, may be true, but it is but a fence around the truth, an approximation. Biographies of Tsvetaeva by Simon Karlinsky and by Veronique Lossky provide only minimal insight into the married life of the Efrons. On the one hand, one is thankful to them, but in this very obscure case, an intimate look could clarify some things, especially because in Tsvetaeva's poetry, love and sexual passion play an important role.

Both Efron as well as Marina are convinced that their marriage can no longer survive. But only days later, each is separately convinced that without their protection the life of the other spouse would be a disaster. So they establish a tacit agreement to not separate. They are fooling themselves, or wish to fool themselves, because they each have a unique ability for survival. The proof is manifest: in all the dire situations they faced during the seven years of separation—war, threats of all kinds, loss of economic security, death by starvation of a daughter, twenty thousand dangers from which they escaped, he on the German front and then in intermittent battles in Crimea where he was threatened by two enemies flanks, the Bolsheviks and the Whites—they had managed to come out alive and in perfect physical shape, or close; and now he was studying philology with a scholarship from the Czechoslovakian government, and she had emerged as a first-rate literary figure; when they have lived through all that and are fully active, the argument to not separate, to not leave the other unprotected, rings false, trivial. For her, the frequent romantic crises meant a subsequent rebirth, from each disastrous story a bundle of splendid poems was born. The covenant established in Prague was maintained until the end. Ultimately, the solution was the worst, the most ruthless they could invent. Neither party ever moved out of the house, but who knows what amount of lost energy, of limitations, were left rotting at their core, what toxins accumulated. Sergei was forced to play the role of the offended party. In the intellectual circle of Russians in Prague everyone learned about the acute marital crisis. Marina announced her unbridled passion for a second-rate Casanova and the women of the circle intensified their sympathy for the aggrieved husband and their coldness for his wife. Might their commiseration have been humiliating for him? Could it have given him some satisfaction? It was, in the eyes of the others, like this: the hero, who took up arms for the restoration of order, was deceived by a terrible woman; the young officer whom his friend betrayed, was seduced by a black sheep, a nasty, pompous, and extravagant shrew. With Efron it is difficult to know. Soon after, a new son was born, Georgy, whom Marina, from the first moment, desperately loved, isolated from the world, wrapped in cellophane, and declared her property in full. In a blurry photo on a wooden staircase in a visibly miserable place, an old woman is seen, sitting next to a blond boy. The photograph is dated 1935, so the child would have been barely ten, but his appearance is that of an adolescent, the Russian athletic type, with the scowl of someone who has few friends; the woman at his side, disheveled, shaken, watches the photographer with a look of anxiety and something akin to despair. They are, as you have probably already guessed, Marina Tsvetaeva and Georgy Efron, the famous Mur. Her biographers, the chroniclers of Russian exile, all agree that the mother had erected an invisible fence around him from which it was difficult for the child to escape; she adored him, spoiled him, was proud of him, but she could not let him breathe outside her reach. He was entirely hers. The quality of the photograph is poor, and the reproduction worse. It is incommensurate with a scene of familial plenitude, of harmony between mother and son. Looking at her, we already know that Mur gives the orders and the old distraught woman, who believes she is the mistress, is in fact the victim. The young Theseus and the Minotaur, which, by way of an extravagant metamorphosis, has been transformed into a chimera. It's a terrible time for Tsvetaeva; she lived in poverty after arriving from Paris, which was increasingly exacerbated by attacks from all sides. Her situation is in sharp contrast to the other two family members who, sitting in a forest, have achieved harmony in their friendship. Their ideas are the opposite of Marina's. They have become, like many people in France, in Europe, in the entire world, since the economic crisis of 1929, pro-Soviet.

The most difficult personality to discern is Efron. He begins projects that he never finishes. His wife's friends believe him to be unintelligent. He seems not to be interested in what they think of him. Surely by today his file in the Lubyanka has cleared up all the mysteries that surround him. All the parts that form the puzzle are classified there. But just thinking about him, he becomes a very suggestive fictional character. It is possible that his older sisters, who raised him after the suicide of his mother and older brother, and the associated trauma, may have turned him into a dependent being, a superfluous man like so many good and wretched men who populate the Russian literary world, that he feared loneliness, that he preferred to endure all the humiliations that his elders before him, and his wife later, inflicted on him in exchange for allowing him to live in their shadow. She had become one of the great figures of exile and he had come to nothing. Mirsky already by the early twenties added a page on her poetry to the splendid history of Russian literature that he published in England. Her fame grew rapidly; she had to her credit a dozen books of poetry, Czechoslovakia had been for her a fertile space for creation. Apparently, however, nothing about the country or its culture interested her, because she was more deeply rooted in its language and German literature was only of secondary interest. She was ready to take the plunge: Paris. It is possible that such circumstances were pleasing to her husband, but it is also possible that he concealed inside himself a seed of rancor without even being aware of its existence. The result would manifest itself as a dead weight for the family: leaving everything unfinished, like his studies in Moscow, his philology studies in Prague, and later his film studies in Paris. His wife would be famous; he would applaud her thunderously at the end of her readings. His wife would sleep with whomever she liked, and would maintain via correspondence platonic relationships with the brightest luminaries in Europe; he, meanwhile, would read newspapers and converse with his daughter, with whom he was growing increasingly closer. He freed Marina so she could depart for Paris, where he would join her months later, so she could settle in to her liking and occupy her rightful place. Recognition awaited her, and in the first months she received it. It was enough that Dmitri Svyatopolk-Mirsky declared in his journal the primacy of Tsvetaeva above all poets in exile, and that she wrote a literary article, in which she demonstrated that the exiled Russians critics were incapable of judging the new poetry, for her to be anathematized by almost the entire Russian community in France. Her arrogance did the rest. Sergei Efron would arrive in Paris later and would be invited by Svyatopolk-Mirsky and some other intellectuals to edit a magazine of Russian culture, a culture different from that of exile, and different above all from how it was conceived in Paris' Russian circles. For them no one who had stayed in the Soviet Union deserved the name of writer, much less a poet. They were nothing but trash, rabble, like Eisenstein in film, like Meyerhold in theater. The Svyatopolk-Mirsky and Efron magazine took at its name the title of a book by Tsvetaeva: *Milestones*. That closeness was enough for the writer to be regarded by the most narrow-minded as a voice in the service of the Bolsheviks. She, who in her public appearances continued to read some of the hymns to the White Guards! As early as 1927, after just a year and a half in France, she was already lamenting: "In Paris, with rare personal exceptions, everyone hates me, they write all sorts of nasty things about me. According to them, I write poems in the style of the 'Communist Youth' and I receive a 'salary from the Bolsheviks.'"[17]

While in Paris the Efrons lived in conditions of extreme poverty, in squalid neighborhoods on the city's outskirts; changing residences inevitably meant descending into an even greater squalor. At times, all four slept in one room, without sanitary facilities. And under these conditions, crushed by the needs of the household, she wrote unceasingly. The awareness of her genius never abandoned her. The intense correspondence she maintained with Rilke in 1926, and the elegy that he wrote for her shortly before his death, were for her the highest praise that her effort deserved:

> Waves, Marina, we're ocean! Depths, Marina, we're sky!
> Earth, Marina, we're earth, thousand times Spring,
> the larks which an outburst of song flings toward the
> Invisible! We begin it as jubilation, from the first it
> wildly exceeds us![18]

That Rilke would sing her in one of his great elegies sheltered her from the cawing rooks who insulted her. By 1933, all sectors were against her: the Communists for her boundless praise of the old Russia, the crown, the Tsar and his family; and conservatives, on

---

17   I was unable to find the entire quote in English translation. The first sentence was translated by Elaine Feinstein. —*Trans.*

18   Translated by Edward Snow.

the other hand, for her admiration of Pasternak and Mayakovsky. Simon Karlinsky notes, "She had gone too far for the left and right at the same time. In the end no one spoke to her." At the very end of their stay in France, Efron began working in a Soviet office of repatriation of Russian exiles, which left no doubt in the minds of the Russian exiles regarding his activities.

And then the big surprise! The body of a Soviet agent who had defected was found in Lausanne. One of the murderers was arrested. There were witnesses that saw him on different occasions enter the office of repatriation where Sergei Efron worked. Efron is summoned to a police station for questioning, after which he disappears and reappears months later in Moscow, where Ariadna was already living. Soviet intelligence services organized his flight to protect him, it was said, fearing perhaps that he would give details about the case, and perhaps about others. Would it not seem that the direction his life had taken was revenge, even if unconscious, for the humiliation he suffered years ago in Prague, for the accumulation of grievances, for the scorn in which Marina held him in every sphere, intellectual and sexual?

As Sergei and Ariadna moved increasingly closer toward Communism, Marina wrote relentless tributes to the Whites. The first, *The Demesne of the Swans*, was followed by another that had been conceived in Paris, *Perekop*, a long dark poem about the last battle fought by those crusaders who fascinated her so much and their final surrender in Perekop; in her final years she took notes to write a long elegy in memory of the Tsar's family, of which only fragments remain. The two halves of the marriage gradually radicalized their positions. During her last period in Paris, she was no longer able to publish. For the first time, she began to feel devalued and out of place. The few letters she sent to distant friends reflect her disenchantment. Her housing conditions were atrocious, sordid rooms in squalid hotels; alone, she began to feel that even poetry itself was abandoning her. And in this condition of delirium, seeing no outlets in France, without friends, without means of subsistence, she committed the biggest mistake of her life: she returned to Russia, to live in a society that she hated and where she was hated, where she reunited with her family, a few friends from her youth—Ehrenburg, Pasternak, Prince Svyatopolk-Mirsky, who had converted to Marxism and repatriated—her sister Anastasia, her sisters-in-law and, above all, Sergei and Ariadna. She lived with her husband and daughter only a few weeks, later both were arrested, as well as her sister Anastasia, and for two years she led a ghostly life in Moscow, a shadow of other shadows. Mur rebels. He accused her of being responsible for the family's misfortunes, for his father's and sister's imprisonment, for the absence of destiny that is being constructed for him. Then came the war, and she committed suicide.

In her lifetime, some of those who dealt with her, loved and admired her, were amazed by the conspiracy that existed between her genius and her inability to perceive reality.

Pasternak, one of her closest friends, sketched some features of Marina in his *An Essay in Autobiography*:

> That Marina Tsvetaeva had always held her work between herself and the reality of daily life; and when she found this luxury beyond her means, when she felt that for her

son's sake she must, for a time, give up her passionate absorption in poetry and look around her soberly, she saw chaos, no longer screened by art, fixed, unfamiliar, motionless, and, not knowing where to run for terror, she hid in death, putting her neck into the noose as she might have hidden her head under her pillow.[19]

---

19   Translated by Manya Harari.

28 MAY

At the Iveria Hotel. I've been in Tbilisi one full day. My room is on the seventh floor. The view is superb. I did a vast number of things today and I feel tired. Yesterday, I still didn't know if I would come to Georgia. But I sent word to the literary chieftains that I was fed up with their vagueness and their mysteries, so the best thing to do would be to interrupt my trip though the USSR and return to Prague. I was given to understand that would happen, but a short time later a ticket to, yes, Tbilisi arrived by messenger, an employee from the bottom of the hierarchy, or so he referred to himself; I don't know whether to apologize or scold myself for my thanklessness, because they had bestowed so many kindnesses on me and I had not responded in kind, I was now getting what I deserved, that is, his humble company. Even on the plane I found it hard to believe that I was heading to Tbilisi, *Tiflís* in Spanish (an obsolete name, even in Spanish publications the Georgians write Tbilisi), where I arrived at ten at night, replete with a splendid moon. Sensation of treading on royal ground! From what I was able to glimpse by moonlight, it is a splendid city, different from all other Soviet cities. Today I started my tour, I began to touch the strata that make it up, a constant process of mental construction or deconstruction, a trip through various cultural layers that have been superimposed on the region, leaving vestiges of what it has been: Hellas, Byzantium, Persia, the Slavs of the first millennium, the Christian churches of the fifth century, the influence of Central Asia, Sufism. Visually, bathed in evening light, Tbilisi is an Andalusian town nestled in the Caucasus. The Persian presence is equivalent to the Arab presence in Andalusia. By day it has other attributes, a majestic topography, a city of hills and canyons crossed by a river that can be seen from everywhere. The houses appear to rush toward the void, terraces and balconies fly through the air, over cliffs, through which flows the mighty Kura. I was just with the writers at their organization's headquarters. They are truly the rebellion; at least the handful with whom I spoke. They have invited me to a banquet, a *supra*, at two in the afternoon. Last night, after arriving at the airport, I knew my stay in Georgia would be wonderful. Despite recent disappointments and inconveniences, I can say that it has been a memorable journey, and that the obstacles to reach my goal had a noticeable effect: they caused my interest in the region to grow. In *The Tempest*, Prospero magically devised an intricate plot so that Miranda, his daughter, and the heir to the kingdom of Naples will fall in love. It is the first step towards the unmasking of his enemies and their asking for forgiveness for having dethroned and exiled him. Many years have passed, and it is time to repair the wounds. The young couple's love, and their subsequent marriage, is the bond that reunites the separated parties. It was enough that the two young lovers look into each other's eyes to become bewitched. Prospero is happy because this event is an essential part of his strategy, but, as an intelligent man, he decides to thwart the lovers' conversation, punish their love, knowing that when the triumph of love is easy, its value decreases. If they had read Shakespeare well, Russian writers would not have placed so many obstacles and difficulties in my way to reach Georgia. Their strategy was wrong. They destined that I find all the virtues of the world in this place. At the airport, I already noticed that the standard of living is much higher than the two major Russian cities: Moscow and Leningrad. As soon as I left the airport my sinusitis disappeared. And throughout the morning I have breathed beautifully.

29 MAY

Into what world have I stumbled? Last night I couldn't write anything about my visit to the Writers' House, my walks, the *supra* on the riverbank, and something else that I find hard to describe. In the morning, I continued to enjoy the splendid view that the balcony affords me. I had already spent a while there before bathing. The climate is perfect, like Cuernavaca's. Around the hotel, brick houses of two or three stories with red roofs abound, which contrast with the architecture of cement or reinforced concrete that is now fashionable in the world and is abused in socialist countries. In the distance, all around, towers with conical metal roofs dot the landscape. Some buildings with Moorish elements, possibly from the last century, with a more or less artificial appearance, stand out. The towers of the Orthodox churches and monasteries have the air of minarets trimmed mid-growth. Yesterday, an interpreter, who will be my guide to take me to the Writers' House, came to pick me up. I walked into a room where there were a dozen Georgians; a few more arrived later. On the tables there are big ceramic bowls overflowing with fruit. During our conversation we are invited to eat giant pears and apples; they peel them with knives in slow, precise gestures, cut them elegantly, and ceremoniously offer each other pieces of fruit as if fulfilling an ancient rite, then offer them to me and my guide. I learn that the first book of literature written in Georgian dates to the fifth century, an extremely remote date, and their ecclesiastical literature is even older. I ask them to repeat the date for me, because it seems all but impossible that the Georgians already had books in their language in the final days of the Roman Empire, five centuries before the Romance languages had produced a literary text. Could it have been the fifteenth century? I ask again, and they answer no. They also explain to me that the golden age of Georgian literature was the twelfth century, in which the great classic of the nation, *The Knight in the Panther's Skin*, was composed by Shota Rustaveli. I gather from the conversation that Georgian literature as well as cinema and theater are based on three elements: a strict sense of form, an effort of imagination that in no way dismisses the mythological, an attachment to reality, and at the same time the criticism of that very reality. They repeatedly complain that for a long time Georgians have not been considered as thinking beings, but rather as a national group that expresses its happiness vacuously by singing, dancing, and drinking wine all the time. "For many it has been very eye-opening to know that we Georgian writers and filmmakers are tremendously self-critical. We are not only a hedonistic nation, it must be stressed, but also a tragic one," says the writer who chairs the meeting. Another man, in his sixties, short, plump, with a sensual mouth and skin that has been cruelly punished by smallpox, or by juvenile acne so pernicious that it destroyed his face, protests in a muffled voice, because the fair sex, the blessed ladies, above all the Nordic and German ones, consider Georgians as mere sex objects and not as subjects capable of making poetry, and this had ruined the prestige of the nation. "Pasternak was a great enthusiast of our poets, he wrote about them and translated the best. The French translations have been based on his translations, they have been published in France and Switzerland, and it has been very difficult to get out of their head that their splendor is owed to Pasternak alone and not to the authors themselves, whom they regard as mere raw material. But what can we do, their wives, their daughters come to Georgia and when they return to their countries what they want to talk about is the muscular strength of our boys, what they have between their legs, and not that they read poems here or there. They come in the summer, not like lobsters—not at all!—they come like packs of cougars, and they pounce hungry and ferocious on our defense-less bodies; not even the old men are safe. We endure them for three months during summer, and they leave us looking like skel-etons. Our brains dry up and it takes us a long time to recover our vitality and remember our language properly. There is a lack of respect in such a crude way of behaving, don't you think? One of my cousins who is older than I, his legs amputated in the war…" And there they all stop him mid-gallop. He acts a little stunned, apologizes, everyone then laughs, they talk among each other, discuss something that the interpreter doesn't want to translate for me, peel more apples and pears, cut them into pieces and share them again. "Perhaps," says a playwright, Shadiman Schamanadze, the youngest of the group, "no country in the world feels dissat-isfaction for its achievements like Georgia. They label what amazes them about us as experiments in the avant-garde, we're either the children of Beckett, or the surrealists or the minimalists; okay, yes, some may be, but I think we are instead the result of a different tradition, which goes far back in time." Someone explains that the new generation feeds on ancient Georgian literature, and that's why it seems so new. "What is being written today," the playwright insists, "is a tragic literature, characterized by its acceptance of pain. The recognition of a moral code that comes from antiquity. What differentiates us from the West," he concludes, "is our wish to build." Before leaving the Writers' House they showed me a list of Mexican books translated into Georgian in the last ten years: Rafael Muñoz's *Let's Go with Pancho Villa*; *The Underdogs* by Mariano Azuela; and *The Death of Artemio Cruz,* by Carlos Fuentes, along with some ghosts of socialist realism, which nobody in Mexico reads—least of all the left: Lorenzo Turrent Rozas, José Mancisidor and others…I then had a few hours to begin my city tour and my rudimentary apprenticeship about things in Georgia. In the year 337 (the source comes from museum brochures), Christianity was officially accepted in Iberia (Eastern Georgia), that is, surprisingly long before Rome. Its great religious art flourished from the eighth to the eleventh century. They showed me wonderful icons, in one of them St. George slays the Emperor Constantine with a spear, evidently before his conversion to Christianity. A linguistic relationship has been found between Georgian and the Basque language. One of the oldest names of the region was Iberia. This first day in Georgia was equivalent in intensity to a quarter of my usual life. What a radiant representation of life! What faces, what eyes, what movements while walking, what voices! No praise is enough to describe them. It would certainly be sparing. What is most striking is their naturalness. These are people who have made great strides. The street shows it. The women and the men, the old and the young, all seem to own the space in which they were destined to live, perhaps the entire world. The group that met at the restaurant at noon was made up of the writers I met in the morning plus a few others, as well as visual artists. There were several very beautiful young women whom no one was able to identify for me, whether wives or daughters of the attendees, or writers or actresses; the truth is, they all looked like actresses of a single role, that of *Carmen la de Triana*. I compare this encounter to the lunch with the Muscovite "writers," who seemed like somber mummies, pompous caricatures compared to the flesh and blood people with whom I am meeting now. Before eating I made a short speech of gratitude. I spoke of the happiness I had noticed in the city, and concluded by saying only that a State that succeeded in bringing happiness to its people, that had at hand the resources to meet the physical and spiritual needs of society, justified a political and social system. The same young playwright from that morning replied that I shouldn't let the solar aspect of this Southern country fool me, that Georgians were far from being the swarm of voluptuous heathens that the world reveled in seeing, but rather thinking people, serious and critical of their own shortcomings. I liked his answer, but by then I rejoiced in everything that was being said at the table. It was a Pantagruelian banquet that lasted five hours. Solemn at moments but always entertaining. The villain of every story was socialist realism—its mere mention provoked uproarious laughter. Both malicious and humorous anecdotes were recounted

of some literary figures from Soviet Central Asia, local heroes who
in their youth had written poems or novels, and who in recent
decades did nothing but write speeches at conferences like the
one that was being prepared. Bottles of an almost black wine were
circulated endlessly. There was a moment when everyone was
talking without knowing to whom. My interpreter translated into
French loose phrases here and there, words that did not connect
with anything, or instead of translating things that interested me,
he described instead the gestures and movements of the characters,
which made me feel on stage acting in a piece by Ionesco: "What
did the young lady who made everyone laugh say?" I asked, and
he replied: "That woman is not as young as you might think, she
ended up sitting down, look, she finally took the spoon to her
mouth," or, in response to the question about what the director
of the Union said during his toast, he said: "The *tamada* raises the
horn of plenty with his right hand; his neighbor was served caviar
and now he's running his hand along his jacket sleeve to remove
the crumbs." "But what is the *tamada* saying at this moment?"
I insisted. "He is saying that nature is taking revenge on us, and
with each passing day the revenge will be greater. Look at the
woman there, across from us, she's an architect, although she
doesn't look like one. They are serving grape leaves stuffed with
ground beef again. He's talking about a confusion of the sexes,
because an American woman who was here recently combed her
hair like a cowboy and didn't allow anyone to call her *girl* but
rather *boy*, and used the masculine gender; she said, for example,
'We Oklahoma boys…'" I began to speak in very bad Russian
with another table companion. I think I understood that Bob

Dylan and some friends, one of which was the woman who insisted she was a *boy*, had eaten with them very recently at the same restaurant, as guests of Yevgeny Yevtushenko, and are probably at his villa right now, on one of the famous beaches: Batumi and Sukhumi, places I'd like to visit one day as a tourist. I glanced across the table and saw that the *supra* had taken on an air of bedlam. They've added tables and chairs and the group was becoming immense, we had taken over the entire terrace, at times the musicians approached us, played their instruments beside us, and everyone sang beautifully and endlessly. The laughter was explosive and contagious. Against all warnings from Dr. Rody, my physician in Prague, I drank like a fish without feeling the slightest discomfort. At times, I was annoyed by the excessive nationalism of some of the dinner guests; it seemed like as the liquor took over the sense of race grew, which caused me to make scenes, to quote Thomas Mann and mention his concept of citizen of the world. And when they squawked about the purity of their blood, I sang the praises of *mestizaje*, I reminded them that Pushkin was a mulatto and toasted to him. The protocol, the very conception of the Georgian *supra*, does not favor two-way communication. Only the *tamada*, the toastmaster, can concede the floor, and on this occasion it was the director of the Writers' Union, a man of great stage presence and whose authority was accepted by the others. Every time I tried to participate, he allowed me to say four or five words, six at the most, then cheerfully interrupted me to allow someone else to tell a story in which everyone participated alternately with a comment. Of course, one could always talk privately with those at the table, but not for long. The unfolding of a Georgian meal can be both thrilling and fatiguing. The table must always be scrved, glasses filled, and the environment must remain lively and cordial. The hosts are princes…I started to feel fatigued, I desperately needed to urinate and wash my face, bathe it, soak my head, so I looked for the men's room. A female employee made it known that on that day it was closed, she showed me a sign and told me in Russian that I should go down beside the river, where I'd find the great *toilette*. The pockmarked writer changed seats and sat next to me. Using macaronic Italian he continued to tell me about the persecutions in which he had been an object during the summers; soon he would retire to the mountains, to a village that is difficult to access, where it would be calmer, he would go with other old men to rest, or rather to hide, because last year he had to live locked in a barn where his grandchildren smuggled him food, "Because the German and Finnish women climb like goats, I swear, I'm convinced they would climb the Himalayas if they knew they would find a lost Georgian man there, and even if he were dying, they'd bang him, just imagine what they'd do in places that aren't as inaccessible; they're guided by smell, they say that the semen of the Georgians is gold; bah, nonsense, but that's what they say, and that it's also the most aromatic in the world, so they go around like little animals sniffing the ground, rooting for truffles, by the aroma alone, that's how they are." He offered to go with me to the restroom and bring me back to the restaurant. It is impossible for me to write more. The experience was almost traumatic, it was too disturbing, the smell of excrement makes me physically ill, and I had had tons to drink. I left the toilet alone and arrived back at the restaurant as best I could to find my guide to take me to the hotel, I think I didn't even say goodbye to any-one. I'll have to apologize. A very beautiful young woman stopped me to tell me that the man who went outside with me was her father, and that he had not returned. She asked me if he had said whether he was going straight home. I said I didn't know, but that he had left, that I saw him leave. "To the right or left?" she wanted to know. I replied that I hadn't noticed, that it seemed instead that he had gone to the river. If I had been honest, I would have had to tell her that the last place I left him was at the latrine, and that he was lowering his pants while talking to some boys who welcomed him with obvious delight.

30 MAY

Back to yesterday. I arrived at the hotel very tipsy thanks to the barrels of red wine I ingested. The spectacle left me quite disturbed. It was, above all, a blow to modesty. Since childhood I have shuddered at seeing such bodily activities. I have spent my entire life avoiding them. Witnessing such an unexpected excremental jamboree rattled me. More than the stench, what really upset me was the ease with which these functions were performed. I imagine that the writer who had been plagued by the insatiable rut of females from the West offered to accompany me to the toilet to reduce the effect had I entered the place alone. We left the restaurant, walked down the street stairs that led to the river, and before reaching the embankment we entered a small door. It seems that there wasn't even a sign on the outside, although I'm not sure. The truth is that it was not a secret place, quite the opposite! As soon as I crossed the threshold, I felt a strong blow to my stomach, lightheadedness, a repulsive gust of putrid air. We went down yet another flight of stairs to reach a vast space. By the din that was heard, the locale must have been very crowded. Perhaps the city's central latrine. The light was very low.

At one point I could glimpse through the fetid mist a long row of men of all ages, sitting on a never-ending bench. It was a collective latrine, something I would never have imagined existed, outside correctional facilities, if even there. A few were trying to read the paper, others were talking or debating. My companion said that it was a soccer game day, that's why there was so much hubbub. He turned to greet someone. On the other side of the giant room a metal canal ran from wall to wall: the urinal, toward which I headed. There was no collective shame. Belly laughs could be heard intermingled with belly noises. The cavernous stench was unbearable. I was afraid that I was going to faint. I looked for that insane pockmarked Virgil that had led me to that fecal circle of hell to ask him to get me out of there immediately, and I saw him happy, as if he had arrived at the agora at the zenithal moment, chatting happily with some boys and greeting others while he unbuttoned his pants and headed to one of the holes to defecate. I left as best I could, I got to the restaurant, I asked the guide to take me in a taxi to the hotel and fell in the bed like a log. I awoke, as I said, I think, queasy, bathed, and changed clothes, as the scenes I had witnessed danced in my head like a vague and distant memory, isolated fragments of a nightmare. I decided not to be dramatic about it. The aspirin had already taken its effect. I drank a couple of espressos in the hotel and started to walk along the Rustaveli, the city's main avenue. I arrived at the theater of the same name, and remembered the fabulous representation of *Richard III* by Shakespeare that the company from the theater had performed at the Cervantes Festival about three or four years ago. A production that had a bit of more radical German Expressionism, with popular marionettes, very colorful, with very marked features, gestures, and movements. The theater is surrounded by a wooded park. I walked along a path. Spring was at its best. The trees were beginning to bloom and the aroma was wonderful, the scent of… I was going to say peach, I think, but suddenly to my astonishment, I open my mouth and say aloud: *"Sal mojón / de tu rincón / hazme el milagro / niño cagón."*[20] I repeated this refrain two or three times, and caught a glimpse of a courtyard, next to a staircase, or in its landing, with big pots of white hydrangea, sitting on a little chamber pot, my pants around my ankles, and a servant girl, still almost a child herself, who was repeating these verses over and over again, teaching me to defecate in that specific place and not in my clothes. It must be the earliest memory, or one of the two most distant I've been able to rescue from my memory. How old could I have been? Three, at most four. I recited it again. I was in Puebla, at my aunt and uncle's house, where we lived for a while. Everything was neat, transparent—I was surrounded by happiness. My mother must have been somewhere upstairs in one of the rooms, and my *tía* Querubina and my cousins Olga and Lilia, who were almost the same age as my mother, and my father was probably still alive; everything was joy, yes, but mostly it was emptying my bowels at that moment and repeating the words the girl is teaching me and hitting my thighs with my fists to the rhythm of the words, and *mamá* is surely waiting for me and will hug me as soon as she sees me in the doorway, she will sit me on her lap, kiss me because the girl will tell her that I had already gone on

20 "Come out turd / from your corner / do me this miracle / little shitting boy."

the potty. "Cannot bear very much reality. / Time past and time future / What might have been and what has been / Point to one end, which is always present."[21] A happiness embraced me in that park that surrounded the Rustaveli Theatre, and I emerged from the spell and noticed that such a memory would not have been revealed if not for the shock suffered hours ago. I left the park, I paused in front of the theater to see the programs of the month and the photos of the new productions, and later I arrived at the hotel and had another coffee and toast and went back to my room and remembered the woman who attended my lecture on *The Mangy Parrot* by Fernandez de Lizardi at the Library of Foreign Languages in Moscow, who told me about the anthropological studies of her husband, of the festivals of spring where they worship a *niño cagón*, a shitting child, or something like that, and I then established a comparison between that woman and another one I saw many years ago in a restaurant in Istanbul, who suddenly began to sing "Ramona," the song from the twenties interpreted by Dolores del Río, and their faces overlapped, and I knew then I was about to write a novel that would bring all this together when I arrived in Prague.

Today, during the day, I have seen splendid corners of Tbilisi, I left town, I have seen wonders, I have spoken with interesting people, eaten delicious food, drunk wines as dark as dreams, and dreamt visions of drunkenness. My approach to all these activities is real, but there also lives in me the project of the *novel of the lower bodily stratum*. I long to get to Prague, to the shelf where Bakhtin's

---

21   Pitol is quoting T.S. Eliot's poem "Burnt Norton" from his *Four Quartets.* —*Trans.*

book on the carnival and functions of the lower bowel in the popular culture of the late Middle Ages and early Renaissance is located. The woman from the library and the Turkish woman who sang at the café in Istanbul will be the same person, a woman from the Caucasus: a Georgian or an Armenian. Perhaps the narrator comes to Tbilisi, or to the sophisticated Georgian spas on the Black Sea, Sukhumi or Batumi, and visits this woman who cares for her husband's papers as if they were a treasure. There should be some ambiguity as to the character of the anthropologist; he could be a genius or a charlatan, that ambiguity that always exists when widows speak of their dead husbands: they are capable of exalting impressive nincompoops, because doing so gives them importance, fame, status, they know that the world is convinced that behind every great man is a great woman, and over time they force the process along, by constructing a virtual edifice they speak of how the main idea arose, which made the deceased famous, and they modestly suggest that it came from a marital conversation, or from something she once said, a sudden moment of truth she had in the kitchen or bathroom, or in the park, perhaps it was a triple moment of truth and when she spoke of it with her husband, a light bulb came on in his brain and he began to work in that particular direction, which she pointed to, and at the very end, in old age, after many years of widowhood, she regretted having married a man who was good and generous, but was also limited, mediocre most of all, because what little he did was thanks to her, yes, of course, but if he had had talent, if he had come to understand what she was, by at least attempting to understand her, he would have become an Einstein, a Nietzsche, a Borges.

Anyway, it would be interesting to investigate what was really the impression this female character I'm thinking about had of her husband: her name will be Marietta, Marietta Karapetian. And I know she must have a foil, an enemy, perhaps secret, throughout her life. And the central part of the novel will be about her trip to the Mexican jungles with her husband and the celebration of spring with a fecal feast in which an infant participates as the final character. And in the story's plot, in the language's substratum will be, of course, a snapshot of the latrine in Tbilisi, but without ever mentioning it in the novel. Someone, her husband, or perhaps her foil or several of their friends, will refer to her as the *la Divina Garza,* the Divine Heron.[22]

While dining with some Georgian journalists I related the incident at the restaurant at the Writers' House years before, when Akhmadulina arrived, at a difficult time, on the arm of the Minister of Culture of the Republic of Georgia, and the security that this afforded her. "Ever since then we've felt here the need to open windows, to let in fresh air. We knew that the time would come, that we were getting close, and that if we did not act in time we would lose it." He explains to me that the current Minister of Foreign Affairs Eduard Shevardnadze was at the time the leader of the Communist Party in Georgia, the strong man, that is. Shevardnadze developed a proto-perestroika on a local level over ten years ago. With few statements and firm action a culture was stimulated closer to that of Poland or Hungary than to the

---

22   Pitol here is referring to a Mexican expression, "*creerse la divina garza*" [to think oneself the divine heron], which he would subsequently use in the title of his novel, *Domar a la divina garza* [Taming the Divine Heron]. An English equivalent would be "queen bee." —*Trans.*

prevailing culture in the USSR. And this was possible thanks to good economic management, to the quotas reached, and to a cautious but at the same time absolute policy, subtle but bold. It seems very difficult, but it has been achieved. Shevardnadze is perhaps the closest politician to Gorbachev, who enjoys his greatest confidence. "And the population supports this political and social transformation?" I ask. "I think so, for several reasons. The Stalinists, who constitute the hardest, most visceral enemy front, have not spoken out against it. I think they envision autonomy, independence as a long-term solution. To leave the Federation and establish an independent Georgian state, a republic or a monarchy, it doesn't matter to them; they have grown tired of the Russians, they felt deeply betrayed after the Twentieth Party Congress. Georgia was decimated by Stalinism; and, yet, the people did not believe the crimes denounced by Khrushchev. The situation here was extremely delicate. It was a miracle that a revolution did not erupt. Revolts, yes, sometimes bloody, but inconsequential. Now we'll see. The future is open. What will it bring us?"

I've toured museums, a few churches, Georgia's artistic treasures. Its medieval and Renaissance painting. The Byzantine painting is of exceptional quality, comparable to the pieces by Rublev in northern Russia. Yesterday afternoon I traveled to the old capital, where there are two magnificent churches: one, the Jvari Monastery, boasts a carved stone frontispiece depicting the Ascension of the Cross, carried by two angels, with a lightness that is rarely achieved in stone. The wind has contributed to the deterioration on the faces; below the hair, only the mouth is distinguishable, while all that remains of the other is an eye, which gives the piece an almost abstract character. The other is from the eleventh century: the Svetitskhoveli Cathedral (Saint George?), on whose façade, interwoven in stone, stands a large tree of life. Once inside, one has the feeling of having entered a wide cavern that exists in the core of a mountain. We are a millennium and a half before our time. The lords and the shepherds, warriors all, gathered for devotion to the true faith, the risen Christ, in prayer asking for victory, but something more: the extermination of the Turks, the Persians, of all infidels. The site stretches upward. At the base, there are four angles, which close as the walls rise; in the second bay there are now eight sides and above sixteen, and finally the dome closes on a beautiful crown of thirty two sides. A replica of the Temple of St. George in Jerusalem, they tell me. On one wall there is a large fresco, which no one has been able to date and which contains obvious repairs. Ships abound in it, gliding between mermaids, mermen, and seven-headed hydras. I see no known saints. Everything seems to belong to a different religious order. The Renaissance and Baroque figures of Catholic hagiography—Saint Christopher crossing a river with the child in his arms, Saint Jerome with a book beside a lion, Saint Sebastian tied to a tree, shot with arrows, Saint Lucia showing on a dish her eyes that have been gouged out, Saint Anthony lost in the melancholy of his temptations—do not exist in these heavens. In Orthodox painting female saints hardly exist, or if they do, I did not see them at these sites, nor do I remember any on display during previous visits to the galleries and museums of Moscow. The closest to female saints are the angels, of epicene appearance and almost nonexistent masculinity. There are fiery archangels, armed and warlike, and many other saints on horseback, with helmets and breastplates that cannot be associated with ours from their appearance, dress, or name. A Saint Francis of Assisi here would be the negation of worship. The martial aspect is marked in painting from all periods, and also in the street, in restaurants, wherever you look around the city. What's more, they are one of the longest-living peoples in the world. Russian writers have written about the dignity of the diverse peoples, races, and cultures that populate and flourish in the Caucasus. The attraction of this long mountainous strip of land that runs from the Black Sea to the Caspian has been proverbial, uninterrupted since Pushkin and Griboyedov until today. Taking interest in this region, living with its aborigines has been for them, more than learning and enjoying a physical region rich in scenery, a spiritual experience, and a sentimental education. The Caucasus has long been an exceptionally attractive place for young Russians. Pushkin praises it; somehow he finds there a human nature akin to that of the Gypsies, immaculate, unspoiled by a rigid protocol of education rather governed by instinct. From the children to the elderly, both women and men are nature. Nature within nature. Therefore man there does not fear, as in the North, instinct, nor does he repress it; on the contrary, he makes it his guide. Pushkin spent a few years of his youth exiled, for having written an "Ode to Freedom," in the vicinity of the Caucasus—Bessarabia, in particular—where he wrote one of his first great poems: *The Prisoner of the Caucasus*; and when he turns thirty he undertakes by choice a pleasure trip to Georgia. From Moscow to Tbilisi, on a trip that was described as whirlwind, in twenty-five days. He recalls those days in his diaries as intensely happy. His arrival in the Georgian capital moves him. Upon entering the city he meets a funeral procession guarded by senior Georgian and Russian officers. He asks who the deceased is and whence are they bringing him. And he is petrified to discover that it his friend and contemporary Alexander Griboyedov, a diplomat in Tehran and the author of a sarcastic comedy of an enlightened bent, *Woe from Wit*, which was neither performed nor published during his lifetime, but which the entire Russian intelligentsia knew by heart. The embassy in Tehran was stormed by a mob and the entire staff killed. Pushkin, impressed by the mournful note, reduced his stay in Tiflis[23] to two weeks, barely half the time it takes him to return to Moscow. Pushkin's sexual curiosity had been unsparing since puberty, to the point of becoming a venereal compulsion. The day after arriving in Tiflis, he went to the baths, hoping to relax his muscles from the immense journey; while there, he was surprised to see more than fifty women, both young and old, either in undergarments or completely naked, bathing alongside the men, and that there was no visible sexual swell; the only person distressed was he, but no one seemed to perceive his genital arousal. "I felt as if I had walked into that room like an invisible man," he writes. The young Count Tolstoy, years later, weary from life as a courtesan, throws himself into the Caucasus, and is its captive from the start. The tensions caused by his social life disappear. He has found a land where nature makes the laws and men submit to her and not the other way around. Every human act that is in harmony with nature is no longer a sin. And that natural life is governed by a radiant and vigorous Eros. The Caucasus for him is the land of poetry, truth, and passion. In short, an earthly paradise, a force similar to the first days of creation. The first of Tolstoy's true novels, *The Cossacks*, which he wrote when he was thirty-five, and the last *Hadji Murad*, written at seventy-six, but published posthumously, are set in the Caucasus. They are books of love of the landscapes that astonish him and a devotion to their characters. For him, space and characters in these novels are the same: truth, human dignity. The pilgrimage to the Caucasus, especially Georgia

---

23   Pitol uses Tiflis to allude to the city's historic name and one that Pushkin would have known, to distinguish it from contemporary Tbilisi. —*Trans.*

and Armenia, becomes a literary obligation. Lermontov, Bulgakov, Mandelstam, Pasternak, many others. But it was not all happiness in "the Pearl of Caucasus," as Georgia is ineluctably known in guidebooks. In one of its villages, one of the most feared men who ever lived was born, a demon, Joseph Stalin, the incarnation of evil, who ordered the brutalization, torture, and liquidation of millions of his terrified subjects. If for writers the republics of the Caucasus, Georgia, Armenia, Azerbaijan, and other autonomous regions such as Chechnya and Dagestan were the land of happiness, the relationship with the Russian homeland was visibly less happy and passionate but equally intense. It is a relationship that the pitiful human being, the long-suffering, humiliated Russian, establishes with the sacred. The Russian homeland is Mother. Nature is diminished for the benefit of the mystery of that area which is impossible to capture with reason, rather only with feelings, with the heart, with pity. Cioran, one of the thinkers who has taken the most interest in Russia, wrote: "A people represents not so much an aggregate of ideas and theories as of *obsessions*: those of Russians, whatever their political complexion, are always, if not identical, at least related. A Chaadaev who found no virtue in his country or a Gogol who mocked it pitilessly was just as attached to it as a Dostoevsky. The most extreme of the Nihilists, Nechayev, was quite as obsessed by it as Pobedonostsev, procurator of the Holy Synod and a reactionary through and through. Only this obsession counts. The rest is merely attitude…"[24] I am always excited and surprised by the association of Russia with the body of God. In Leskov's *The Cathedral Folk*, the Russian novelist that

24   Translated by Richard Howard.

Walter Benjamin preferred to other more celebrated writers, a priest is thrilled to learn that a very poor old man, almost a beggar, has taken in an orphan, with whom he shares this scant possessions, and scarcely hearing the news, exclaims: "Oh, you, my beloved Russia, how beautiful you are!" And in the most terrible story one could imagine, *In the Ravine*, by Chekhov, an old man finds a young woman who is carrying her dead son in her arms. He invites her to get in his carriage and tells her:

> "Yours is not the worst of sorrows. Life is long, there will be good and bad to come, there will be everything. Great is mother Russia," he said, and looked round on each side of him. "I have been all over Russia, and I have seen everything in her, and you may believe my words, my dear. There will be good and there will be bad. I went as a delegate from my village to Siberia, and I have been to the Amur River and the Altai Mountains and I settled in Siberia; I worked the land there, then I was homesick for mother Russia and I came back to my native village. We came back to Russia on foot; and I remember we went on a steamer, and I was thin as thin, all in rags, barefoot, freezing with cold, and gnawing a crust, and a gentleman who was on the steamer—the kingdom of heaven be his if he is dead—looked at me pitifully, and the tears came into his eyes. 'Ah,' he said, 'your bread is black, your days are black...' And when I got home, as the saying is, there was neither stick nor stall; I had a wife, but I left her behind in Siberia, she was buried there. So I am living

as a day labourer. And yet I tell you: since then I have had
good as well as bad. Here I do not want to die, my dear,
I would be glad to live another twenty years; so there has
been more of the good. And great is our mother Russia!"
and again he gazed to each side and looked round.[25]

In a single paragraph he has invoked the greatness of Mother
Russia three times! Not only is a Russian susceptible to feeling the
pulse of Mother Russia. Rainer Maria Rilke, whom the Russian
Lou Andreas-Salomé accompanied for several months as a guide,
mother, muse, lover, teacher, writes on July 31, 1900, aboard
a steamer down the Volga, "All that I had seen until then was but
a picture of country, river, world. Here was the real thing in natural size. I felt as if I had watched the creation; few words for all
that is, things made on God the Father's scale."[26] What about that!

---

25   Translated by Constance Garnett.
26   Translated by Margaret Wettlin.

WHEN THE SOUL IS DELIRIOUS

"Paupers, soothsayers, beggars, mendicant chanters, lazars, wanderers from holy place to holy place, male and female, cripples, bogus saints, blind Psalm singers, prophets, idiots of both sexes, fools in Christ—these names, so close in meaning, of the double-ring sugar cakes of the everyday life of Holy Russia, paupers on the face of Holy Russia, holy Psalm singers, Christ's cripples, fools in Christ[27] of Holy Russia—these sugar cakes have adorned everyday life from Russia's very beginnings, from the time of the first Tsar Ivans, the everyday life of Russia's thousand years. All Russian historians, ethnographers, and writers have dipped their quills to write about these holy fools. These madmen or frauds—beggars, bogus saints, prophets—were held to be the Church's brightest jewel, Christ's own, intercessors for the world, as they have been called in classical Russian history and literature. A noted Muscovite fool in Christ—Ivan Yakovlevich,[28] a onetime seminarian—who lived

---

27   Pitol cites here a translator's note to the Spanish translation, which employs the Spanish word "*inocentes.*" The note reads: "The 'innocents' (*yurodivy*) were fools from birth whom the Russian people considered holy, attributing to their words magical and prophetic meanings." —*Trans.*

28   The English translation quoted here includes the following note:

in Moscow in the middle of the nineteenth century, died in the Preobrazhensaya Hospital. His funeral was described by reporters, poets, and historians. A poet wrote in the *Vedomosti*:[29]

> What feast is in the Yellow House[30] afoot,
> And wherefore are the multitudes there thronging,
> In landaus and in cabs, nay e'en on foot,
> And ev'ry heart is seized with fearful longing?
> And in the midst is heard a voice of woe
> In direst pain and grief ofttimes bewailing:
> 'Alas, Ivan Yakovlevich is laid low,
> The mighty prophet's lamp too soon is failing.'

"Stravronsky, a chronicler of the times, relates in his *Moscow Sketches* that during the five days that the body lay unburied more than two hundred masses for the repose of the dead were sung over it. Many people spent the night outside the church. An eyewitness of the funeral, N. Barkov, the author of a monograph entitled *Twenty-six Muscovite Sham Prophets, Sham Fools in Christ, Idiots, Male and Female,* relates that Ivan Yakovevich was to have been buried on Sunday,

---

"Ivan Yakovlevich Koreisha (ca. 1780-1861), for many years as inmate of a Moscow institution for the insane; his followers regarded him as a saint and a seer."—*Trans.*

29   A note to the English translation reads: "*Moskovskiye Vedomosti (Moscow Gazette*), a conservative Moscow daily."—*Trans.*

30   A note to the English translation reads: "Institution for the insane." —*Trans.*

as had been announced in the Police Gazette, and that day
at dawn his admirers began flocking in, but the funeral
did not take place because of the quarrels which broke
out over where exactly he was to be buried. It did not
quite come to a free-for-all, but words were exchanged,
and strong ones they were. Some wanted to take him to
Smolensk, his birthplace; others worked busily to have him
buried in the Pokrovsky Monastery, where a grave had
even been dug for him in the church; others begged tear-
fully that his remains be given to the Alekseyevsky Nun-
nery; still others, hanging on to the coffin, tried to carry it
off to the village Cherkizovo. It was feared that the body
of Ivan Yakovlevich might be stolen.

"The historian writes: 'All this time it was raining, and the mud
was terrible, but nevertheless, as the body was carried from the
lodgings to the chapel, from the chapel to the church, from the
church to the cemetery, women, girls, ladies in crinolines prostrated
themselves and crawled under the coffin.' Ivan Yakovlevich—when
he was alive—was in the habit of relieving himself on the spot:

> He made puddles [writes the historian], and his attendants
> had orders to sprinkle the floor with sand. And this sand,
> watered by Ivan Yakovlevich, his admirers would gather
> and carry home, and it was discovered that the sand has
> healing properties. A baby gets a tummy ache, his mother
> gives him half a spoonful of the sand in the gruel, and the
> baby gets well. The cotton with which the deceased's nose

and ears had been plugged was divided into tiny pieces
after the funeral service for distribution among the faithful.
Many came with vials and collected in them the moisture
which seeped from the coffin, the deceased having died
of dropsy. The shirt in which Ivan Yakovlevich had died
was torn to shreds. When the time came for the coffin to
be carried out of the church, freaks, fools in Christ, pious
hypocrites, wanderers from holy place to holy place, male
and female were gathered outside. They had not gone into
the church, which was packed, but stood in the streets.
And right there in broad daylight, among the assembled,
sermons were preached to the people, visions called up
and seen, prophecies and denunciations uttered, money
collected, and ominous roarings given forth.

"During the last years of his life Ivan Yakovlevich used to order his
admirers to drink the water in which he had washed: they drank it.
Ivan Yakovlevich made not only spoken but also written prophecies
that have been preserved for historical research. People wrote to
him; they would ask, 'Will so-and-so get married?' He would reply,
'No work—no supper…'

"Kitai-gorod[31] Moscow was the cheese in which the fools in
Christ—its maggots—lived. Some wrote verse; others crowed like
roosters, screamed like peacocks, or whistled like bullfinches; others
heaped foulness on all and sundry in the name of the Lord; still
others knew only a simple phrase which was held to be prophetic

---

31   A note to the Spanish translation reads: "An ancient commercial district
of Moscow." —*Trans.*

and gave the prophet his name; for example, 'Man's life's a dream, the coffin—coach and team, the ride—was smooth as cream!' Also to be found were devotees of dog barking who with their barking prophesied God's will. To this estate belonged paupers, beggars, soothsayers, mendicant chanters, lazars, bogus saints— the cripples of all of Holy Russia; to it belonged peasants and townfolk, and gentry and merchants—children, old men, great, hulking louts, brood mares of women. They were all drunk. They were all sheltered by the onion-domed, sky-blue clam of the Asiatic Russian tsardoms; they were bitter as cheese and onions, for the onion domes atop the churches are, of course, the symbol of oniony life."[32]

BORIS PILNYAK
Mahogany
Ardis, 1993

---

32   Translated by Vera T. Reck and Michael Green.

2 JUNE

The trip is almost over. What a shame! Yesterday I spent a long time sitting on the terrace of the hotel. I made a lot of notes of my stay in Georgia. I went early to the Museum of Fine Arts, just to see the paintings again by Niko Pirosmani, a Georgian painter from the beginning of the twentieth-century, who made a living painting signs for stores, workshops, restaurants, and taverns. Compared to Georgian painting of the period, he is head and shoulders above the rest. But not just in Georgia, his paintings would stand out no matter where they were. He was a great painter, but he never knew it. Sometime in the twenties, old, alcoholic, poverty-stricken, he was discovered by some connoisseurs of art. His most notable paintings revolve around the *supra*, that passion of the Georgians: tables filled with delicacies, wine bottles, dinner guests in ceremonial attitude, like sculptures of themselves, and the small Jewish orchestra at the bottom or to the side. The outlines are powerful; the lines are broad and are one of the most important parts of the structure. Immediately after, I was taken to the airport, and at four in the afternoon, I was walking the streets of Moscow. The return has been sensational. Midsummer, 93 degrees. Last night, I took a stroll through the city center for several hours. This morning the same. I was looking for the house where Dr. Chekhov also saw patients. I got lost, took another route and arrived in the old neighborhood of my old embassy; it was more than worth it. It is a place where art nouveau villas abound—meticulously maintained precisely because they host embassies. I passed the International Bookshop opposite the Italian Embassy—lots of books in Spanish in the windows, most from Seix Barral. Under this sun, I've almost regained color. Fascinating city steeped in literature, only suitable to be appreciated by the person who has returned. I remember Pepe Donoso's excitement when we met beside St. Basil's years ago. And the surprise that I felt when he told me that he felt better here than in Leningrad. Leningrad, on that we both agree, is a city built all in the same period, governed by a unique architectural canon, which imprints on its beauty an unspeakable monotony, an artificiality that lacks the mysteries of Venice, Prague. "Having seen the inside of St. Isaac's," Pepe tells me, "says it all, it revealed another city to me. The emptiness of power." I am so happy to be back! To see and feel the beginning of this resurrection. The city's progress is evident in its cleanliness. They have restored many buildings during my absence and publishers are translating more. Books that just five years ago seemed impossible to imagine in Russia are being published. Musil's *The Man without Qualities*, Woolf's *Mrs. Dalloway* and *To the Lighthouse*, *Brideshead Revisited*, by Evelyn Waugh, *The Sleepwalkers*, by Hermann Broch. Clearly, a new thaw has begun. It's a shame that the same intensity is not present in the fields of Hispanism and Latin-Americanism, one doesn't notice the same intensity! Apparently our literatures do not possess such capable defenders. Inna Terterian, who just died, has written the prologue to the works of Borges. That leaves Vera Kuteishchikova. Maybe there are new young ones I don't know. For now, our literature's time has not yet come, but it is coming. *Hopscotch* will soon appear, as will the Borges volume. In the hotel, I saw on television the opening of the World Cup of Soccer. Our president wasn't allowed to speak; he was interrupted by a vociferous public that shouted over him. I'm making a list of characters in my novel. Three or four groups of families. They all have brothers and sisters, I don't know why, but the plot requires it. Reading Gogol is indispensable. It will be the novel's backbone. Gogol, his biographers, his characters…The key figure has to be the woman, the widow of the anthropologist studying indigenous festivals in Mexico. And I've decided that her existential adversary is an academic who epitomizes all the human miseries I detest: avarice, pettiness, inauthenticity, and other things of this tenor; and that he is (inconceivably) a fan of Gogol. I view it as a tribute to the author of *The Nose* and *The Diary of a Madman*.

FEATS OF MEMORY

"Some twenty years later, I undertook a journey to Lausanne, in order to find the old Swiss Lady who had been first Sebastian's governess, then mine. She must have been about fifty when she left us in 1914; correspondence between us had long ceased, so I was not at all sure of finding her still alive, in 1936. But I did. There existed, as I discovered, a union of old Swiss women who had been governesses in Russia before the revolution. They 'lived in their past,' as the very kind gentleman who guided me there explained, spending their last years—and most of these ladies were decrepit and dotty—comparing notes, having petty feuds with one another and reviling the state of affairs in the Switzerland they had discovered after their many years of life in Russia. Their tragedy lay in the fact that during all those years spent in a foreign country they had kept absolutely immune to its influence (even to the extent of not learning the simplest Russian words); somewhat hostile to their surroundings—how often have I heard Mademoiselle bemoan an exile, complain of being slighted and misunderstood, and yearn for her fair native land; but when these poor wandering souls came home, they found themselves complete strangers in a changed country, so that by queer trick of sentiment—Russia (which to them had really been an unknown abyss, remotely rumbling beyond a lamplit corner of a stuffy back-room with family photographs in mother-of-pearl frames and a water-colour view of Chillon castle), unknown Russia now took on the aspect of a lost paradise, a vast, vague but retrospectively friendly place, peopled with wistful fancies. I found Mademoiselle very deaf and gray, but as voluble as ever, and after the first effusive embraces she started to recall little facts of my childhood which were either hopelessly distorted, or so foreign to my memory that I doubted their past reality."

VLADIMIR NABOKOV
The Real Life of Sebastian Knight
New Directions Publishers, New York, 1941

3 JUNE

Tuesday, my last day in the USSR. I don't know whether it's a holiday, at least for the schools; I seem to be seeing more young people in the street than the day before yesterday, Sunday. Before breakfast I packed my luggage; all that's left is to go back later and pack my medicines, some books, the notebooks I've written in these past days. I walked a little, and visited secondhand bookshops. The one in the lobby of the Hotel Metropol is still wonderful. I love casual encounters, sitting on the bench of a boulevard or in a square, starting up conversations with gossipy old women whom I barely manage to understand, with young people, smoking a cigarette with them, and then, getting up, leaving them dumbfounded at having met a Mexican for the first time. I arranged a meeting with Kyrim in the bar inside the Metropol, the one that looks like an American film noir set, where the mix of visitors never seems to jibe with the hotel or with Moscow. From the first day I went there, years ago, I was fascinated. Who were those Russians and the eccentric foreigners who landed there? These are the questions that never interest political scientists or Kremlinologists, which is why it always bored me to read them or listen to them while dining with them at an embassy. Of course, years later I can think of some very remarkable exceptions: some extremely brilliant Italians and, above all, two Poles without equal: Ryszard Kapuściński, the most educated, intelligent, and penetrating chronicler of the Soviet world; and K.S. Karol, both extraordinarily talented at musing on the wide range of elements and details, without becoming prisoners to the naked facts, those which, by themselves, very rarely constitute the truth. When I worked at the embassy I had the opportunity to hear correspondents from foreign newspapers talk about Soviet society, as if it were equal to the Stalinist era. Kapuściński and Karol know how to read other signs and therefore propose richer and much more pertinent accounts. It was impossible to convince any "specialist" that beneath the surface they were examining there were different currents fighting among themselves, even in the Kremlin itself, like there were throughout the socialist world, except perhaps in Albania and Romania. Now perestroika has shown them a different storyline and again they understand nothing. Buried beneath a deceptively homogeneous surface were varied interests, alliances that were difficult perceive and phobias and brutal hatreds that assumed a monolithic unit. Kapuściński recently stated in an interview that "people, even before perestroika, were accustomed to expressing themselves with silence, not with words, the places they frequented and those they avoided, the way they looked at something, the neutral words in a commentary had their meaning. Despite the contempt and arrogance towards society, power continued to pay attention to the kind of silence that they practiced."[33]

---

33 No English translation of this interview could be found; therefore,

This explains the publication of the authors who had been punished in years past, the classics, so to say, the executed, the silenced,
those exiled to the West. Mandelstam, Pasternak, Akhmatova,
Tsvetaeva, Babel, Bulgakov, Pilnyak, Remizov, Bunin, others—
whose books in Moscow and Leningrad were sold in foreign
currency stores, but that members of writers' unions could acquire
in rubles and at a very low price; and also, and above all, books by
contemporary authors that touched politically thorny issues like
Chingiz Aitmatov's *The White Ship*, or *The House on the Embankment* and *The Old Man*, by Yuri Trifonov, and others that, published
begrudgingly and in limited editions, arrived in the bookstores
where they sold out in less than an hour, but that in the ensuing
days had already been devoured by thousands of readers, and the
Taganka Theater, directed by Yuri Lyubimov with an international
audience, and lines a mile long of Russians in search of tickets to
see the stage version of *The Master and Margarita* by Bulgakov. The
cinema of Klimov and Gherman, and foreign films not announced
anywhere that were projected at ten or eleven at night, in a cinema
without marquees, the façade with no lights, before a discerning
and enthusiastic audience of filmmakers, actors, writers, people of
culture, who found out from friends, who knows how, or the
painters' workshops that one visited to acquire paintings by the
new guard, especially abstracts, and many things that were part of
my daily life when I was a cultural attaché and which foreign
correspondents resented knowing, because it was easier to continue a relentless vision that maintained a Cold War climate. I'm
still working on the outline of my next novel. It will be set in

I have translated from the Spanish. —*Trans.*

several places: Istanbul, Rome, Cuernavaca or Tepoztlán, and somewhere in the middle of the Tabasco jungle. I also have sketches of the characters. From the absurd dreams of the last two weeks and the strange fecal coincidences that coalesced between planes and hotel rooms has emerged a possible title: *Señora la Divina Garza* [The Mrs. Divine Heron]. Ten years ago, a young filmmaker who was married to a Colombian girl spoke to me in Moscow about the trends he perceived in the imagination of his contemporaries, university students or young professionals, artists or scientists, friends of his or cousins, or friends of friends, people with a name, with a familiar face, not the abstraction of surveys, and these trends in order of importance were: a) Berdyaevists, those who followed the Christian thought of Berdyaev; b) Neoslavists, that is right-wing nationalists; c) pluralists, democrats of various shades, one of which he ascribed to; d) Zen-Buddhists; and e) Che-Guevarists; the latter two categories, a minority. I asked him about Trotsky: "Are there no Trotskyists?" And the answer was categorical: "Almost none." "Why?" "Because they think that had he won the ideological struggle, he would have followed the same totalitarian path as Stalin, perhaps without the monster-like brutality. His theses on art and literature have no appeal for us, the military tone is palpable, the brutality of the time, perhaps. Some of us have wondered: How could the Formalists have survived the purges: Shklovsky, Eikhenbaum, and Tinianov, or even the less visible: Tomashevsky, Propp, others? And the only answer one finds is that they were saved thanks to the verbal violence with which they were attacked by Trotsky. It was a safeguard for life. If they were scorned in such a way, they must have had some virtue.

Bukharin, however, executed during the purges following a thunderous trial, for being a Trotskyist, nowadays, I don't know why, is beginning to attract scholars and disciples. Now, many like me talk about memory, about what we hear, I personally have not read Trotsky, ever." Not every Russian reacted like a steamroller; there were those, and more than a few, who were extremely knowledgeable and possessed an exceptional artistic sensibility. All one had to do was go to a concert in Moscow given by a great artist to become infected with the intensity of the reception. One felt as if he were in a temple from the seats, surrounded by a kind of religious halo which came not only from the artist who was performing a piece on stage, but also from the hall, from the breath of the several hundred faithful who followed note by note with all their senses, their intelligence and spirit, the progression of a concert. And at the end came the apotheosis, the asceticism, the mystical union with the mystery. Rarely have I experienced so passionately opera and theater as in the theater of the Moscow Chamber Opera, an insignificant hall lost in a nondescript neighborhood of the city, which didn't even have the right to advertise on billboards, or in newspapers, or to reveal their existence on the face of the building. However, despite the official silence, getting tickets at that venue was an extremely complicated feat. They were bought, and with great difficulty, at least two months in advance. It was not a prohibited place, or underground, or anything of the sort; but its existence was only tolerated. To enter there was akin to feeling like a Christian submerged in the catacombs during times of persecution. It was a sanctuary, a protected space where one went to celebrate a sacred rite. There I saw *The Rake's Progress* by Igor Stravinsky. There was no physical distance between singers, orchestra, and audience, which felt bound by the lack of space and the passion of the moment. I never remember feeling such intense emotion and anguish as in that performance, nor have I felt joy comparable to that I experienced in a hilarious performance of *The Nose*, by Shostakovich, based on Gogol's story, presented at that miniscule theater. All this was possible in such a complex, unreal, Gogolian, Kafkaesque, and Dostoevskian society as was Moscow at the end of Brezhnev. Political scientists turned society into a page without reliefs; their position, usually, was to reduce any phenomenon to the statistical or the ideological. What they said about Brezhnev and Suslov, the terrifying ideologue of the Central Committee, and all that gang of decrepit old men was true; it was also true that there was censorship of many forms and huge deficiencies, but there were also top-notch people, intelligent, refined, imaginative Russians, and also spectacular individuals. Oh, and the question of the soul! The Russian soul! Cioran said: "After the war, Laurence Olivier and his company went to Moscow to perform *Romeo and Juliet*. When the show ended, overwhelmed with emotion, the Russians embraced each other as they would Easter night. That is having a soul." Cioran could say it, but I could not. Some Mexican friends were concerned about my *naïveté*, my *stupidity* when I commented on these phenomena of Russian life. And in Spain it was impossible to open one's mouth. Once, at the end of a tremendously fun party in Barcelona, I mentioned something about the Slavic soul and a dear friend became violently enraged. He insulted me as if I were sugarcoating the brutality of the Gulag, as if I wanted to erect a rose-colored façade to conceal

Stalin's crimes. I don't think I've ever felt so hurt, so unfairly judged. Something similar happened to me at a publishers' lunch in Madrid. Anyway…! Well, things have changed, history has moved on…At the Metropol, Kyrim was already waiting for me. He had prepared a wonderful surprise. He had located some of my friends, most of whom were students of theater who were already in their last year when I lived in Moscow and were beginning to practice their craft playing small roles in training theaters. He made a reservation at the most sophisticated private restaurant that exists in the city today: a spacious dacha with several rooms facing the Novodevichy Convent, in whose cemetery Chekhov's grave can be found. The wide Moskva River provided us a superb view of the monastery and its walls. He had booked them early, due to the little time I had left in Moscow. It was the most pleasant moment of the trip. Everything they said to me, the excitement during the encounter, the immense joy, the laughter, because everyone, ever since I've known them, has been blessed by a tremendous sense of humor, each with a different range; thanks in large part to them, my vision of Russia, its people, its culture was different from that of many other diplomats. At the lunch organized by Kyrim there were fourteen or fifteen friends: two Seryozhas, Oleg, Vitia, Asim, Alyosha, Sonia, Alexandra, some wives or husbands whom I didn't know, and two babies, asleep beside us in their carriages. Aroutioun was missing, the person with the biggest personality, the most worldly, the backbone of the group in the past, the son of a famous actress, grandson and nephew of actors emeriti, of musicians and scholars—in short, part of a famous clan in Armenia; and the two Sashas arrived, one originally from the Caspian Sea, and the other from the Urals. They feel good about life. These young people do at work today what just a few years ago would have seemed utopian. They are full of enthusiasm; fire, I dare say. We talked about Georgia, which for them is sacred ground; they shamed me for not having seen the new films made there these days; for a while, the conversation revolved around Aroutioun, and countless anecdotes came to light as well as signs of pride in being friends with that little genius who had already performed Hamlet and Romeo and the Cid, and the student in *The Cherry Orchard*, and the young symbolist writer of *The Seagull*, and went with the national company of Yerevan to the Edinburgh Festival; but, on the other hand, Oleg, a talented Russian from Estonia, the young leading man of the Riga Theatre, had to emigrate to Moscow, because the Russians were displaced from the Republic of Estonia and the theater was closed, and he is now having a hard time in Moscow. We remembered lots of moments from the past and then, when I said goodbye to them, those overwhelming Russian goodbyes that never end, where there are hugs and tears, and eccentric and sweet exchanges, I felt like an orphan of the world, a stray dog in a hostile world, like that of Bulgakov in *Heart of a Dog*, but also felt an immense happiness to see how happy they are. Walter Benjamin, after a catastrophic love affair in Moscow, disillusioned by many things, considered excessively orthodox and sectarian in his political views there, arrives to his homeland and the first thing he yearns for is human warmth, contact with others. "For someone who has arrived from Moscow," he writes in his diary, "Berlin is a dead city. The people on the street seem desperately isolated, each one at a great distance from the next, all alone in a broad stretch of street…"[34]

 I left Moscow in a torrid heat. Yes, I said that already, I think, 93 degrees in the shade. They just announced over the loudspeaker that the temperature in Prague is 54 degrees. And it's also raining.

---

34 Translated by R. Sieburth.

IVÁN, THE RUSSIAN BOY

My mother had died a few months before; I had started school, in a modest private residence with eight or ten pupils. I had not yet been struck by malaria, so I was able to lead a more or less regular life. We sang almost all the time, but also learned to count, read, draw. We were all happy there, I think. Our teacher's name was Charito; she was very fat, but wonderfully agile for dancing, which she did often. My grandmother gave me a book to practice reading at home; it had probably belonged to my mother as a child. On the first page there was a text with some faces, each framed in a box with words of identification. The page was entitled "Human Races" and contained photos or drawings of children from different places and of different races. One of the children had thick lips and high cheekbones, features that gave him an animal-like appearance, a quality that was reinforced by a thick fur cap, which I assumed was his own hair and which went down past his ears. At the bottom it read: *Iván, the Russian boy*. In the evenings, when the house was immersed in sleep, I would take long walks. It was the offseason, those long months of inactivity immediately following the sugar harvest; the huge factory was at that time empty, except, perhaps, during the few days the machinery was being serviced. In the afternoon there were no workers, only an occasional watchman. If anyone asked me what I was doing there, I inevitably replied that the clock in my house had broken and my grandmother had sent me to check the factory clock. So I would go in. I'd cross the central body of the mill, wander its various naves, leave the buildings, and walk up to a mound of bagasse that was drying in the sun. I don't recall now how I came to know about this solitary place or who showed me my way around the maze blocked at every turn by giant machines. Once there, I would sit down or lie on the warm bagasse. From a normal height, I would stare at a ravine that ended in a wall of mango trees. I knew that behind those trees ran the Atoyac River, the same river in which a few miles down my mother had drowned. No one passed by that place, or on the very rare occasion someone did, I would curl up in the bagasse and pretend that I was mimicking the iguanas and become invisible. One day a boy, about four or five years older than I, showed up. He was a complete stranger. It was Billy Scully, a newcomer to Potrero. Billy was the son of the chief engineer of the sugar mill, and he became, from the first moment, a born leader, though never a tyrant, whom we all admired instantly. Before the strength of his movements and the freedom emanating from his whole being, I felt even smaller. He asked me who I was, what my name was.

"Iván," I replied.

"Iván what?"

"Iván, the Russian boy."

Intuitively, I feel that my intimate relationship with Russia goes back to that distant source. Of course, Billy did not believe me, but he didn't let on. I was a rather odd, very lonely, very capricious boy, I think. My problems with mythomania lasted a few years longer, as a defense against the world. Sometimes, later, after a few drinks, they would reemerge, which angered and depressed me to a disproportionate degree. The only exception was my identification with Iván, the Russian boy, which at times still seems to me to be the real truth.

BIBLIOGRAPHY

AITMATOV, CHINGIZ. Trans. Mirra Ginsburg. *The White Ship.* Crown Publishers, 1972.

BENJAMIN, WALTER. Trans. R. Sieburth. *Moscow Diary.* Harvard University Press, 1986.

BERBEROVA, NINA. Trans. Philippe Radley. *The Italics Are Mine.* Vintage, 1993.

CANETTI, ELIAS. Trans. John Hargraves. Farrar, Straus and Giroux, 1998.

CHEKHOV, ANTON. Trans. Constance Garnett. "In the Ravine." *The Portable Chekhov.* Penguin Books, 1977.

CIORAN, E.M. Trans. Richard Howard. *History and Utopia.* University of Chicago Press, 1998.

FERNÁNDEZ DE LIZARDI, JOSÉ JOAQUÍN. Trans. David L. Frye. *The Mangy Parrot: The Life and Times of Periquillo Sarniento.* Hackett Publishing Co., 2005.

KARLINKSY, SIMON. *Marina Tsvetaeva: The Woman, Her World, and Her Poetry.* Cambridge University Press, 1986.

Letters: Summer 1926: Boris Pasternak, Marina Tsvetayeva, and Rainer Maria Rilke. Trans. Margaret Wettlin, Walter Arndt, and Jamey Gambrell. Yevgeny Pasternak, Yelena Pasternak, and Konstantin M. Azadovsky, eds. New York Review Books, 2001.

MANDELSTAM, NADEZHDA. Trans. Max Hayward. *Hope Against Hope: A Memoir.* Modern Library, 1999.

MEYERHOLD, VSEVOLOD. Trans. John Crowfoot. *Arrested Voices: Resurrecting the Disappeared Writers of the Soviet Regime.* Martin Kessler Books, 1996.

NABOKOV, VLADIMIR. *The Real Life of Sebastian Knight.* New Directions Publishers, 1992.

PASTERNAK, BORIS. Trans. Manya Harari. *An Essay in Autobiography.* Collins and Harvill Press, 1959.

PILNYAK, BORIS. Trans. Vera T. Reck and Michael Green. *Mahogany and Other Stories. Ardis Publishers,* 1993.

TSVETAEVA, MARINA. Trans. J. Marin King. *A Captive Spirit.* The Overlook Press, 2009.

RILKE, RAINER MARIA. Trans. Edward Snow. *The Poetry of Rilke.* North Point Press, 2011.

SERGIO PITOL DEMENEGHI is one of Mexico's most acclaimed writers, born in the city of Puebla in 1933. He studied law and philosophy in Mexico City. He is renowned for his intellectual career in both the field of literary creation and translation, and is renowned for his work in the promotion of Mexican culture abroad, which he achieved during his long service as a cultural attaché in Mexican embassies and consulates across the globe. He has lived perpetually on the run: he was a student in Rome, a translator in Beijing and Barcelona, a university professor in Xalapa and Bristol, and a diplomat in Warsaw, Budapest, Paris, Moscow and Prague. In recognition of the importance of his entire canon of work, Pitol was awarded the two most important prizes in the Spanish language world: the Juan Rulfo Prize in 1999 (now known as the FIL Literary Award in Romance Languages), and in 2005 he won the Cervantes Prize, the most prestigious literary prize in the Spanish language world, often called the "Spanish language Nobel." Deep Vellum will publish Pitol's "Trilogy of Memory" in full in 2015-2016 (*The Art of Flight*; *The Journey*; *The Magician of Vienna*, all translated by George Henson), marking the first appearance of any of Pitol's books in English.

GEORGE HENSON's literary translations include *The Art of Flight* by Cervantes Prize laureate Sergio Pitol and *The Heart of the Artichoke* by fellow Cervantes recipient Elena Poniatowska. His translations of essays, poetry, and short fiction, including works by Andrés Neuman, Leonardo Padura, Juan Villoro, Miguel Barnet, and Alberto Chimal have appeared in *The Literary Review*, *BOMB*, *The Buenos Aires Review*, *Flash Fiction International*, and *World Literature Today*, where he is a contributing editor. George holds a BA in Spanish from Oklahoma University, an MA, also in Spanish, from Middlebury College, and a PhD in literary and translation studies from the University of Texas at Dallas.

ALVARO ENRIGUE was born in Mexico in 1969. He is the award-winning author of five novels and two books of short stories. In 2007, the Hay Festival's Bogotá39 project named him one of the most promising Latin American writers of his generation. His linked story collection *Hypothermia*, was published by Dalkey Archive in 2014, and his Herralde Prize-winning novel *Sudden Death* will be published by Riverhead in 2016. He lives in New York.

Thank you all
for your support.
We do this for you,
and could not do
it without you.

DEAR READERS,

Deep Vellum is a not-for-profit publishing house founded in 2013 with the threefold mission to publish international literature in English translation; to foster the art and craft of translation; and to build a more vibrant book culture in Dallas and beyond. We seek out works of literature that might otherwise never be published by larger publishing houses, works of lasting cultural value, and works that expand our understanding of what literature is and what it can do.

Operating as a nonprofit means that we rely on the generosity of donors,cultural organizations, and foundations to provide the basis of our operational budget. Deep Vellum has two donor levels, the LIGA DE ORO and the LIGA DEL SIGLO. Members at both levels provide generous donations that allow us to pursue an ambitious growth strategy to connect readers with the best works of literature and increase our understanding of the world. Members of the LIGA DE ORO and the LIGA DEL SIGLO receive customized benefits for their donations, including free books, invitations to special events, and named recognition in each book.

We also rely on subscriptions from readers like you to provide an invaluable ongoing investment in Deep Vellum that demonstrates a commitment to our editorial vision and mission. Subscribers are the bedrock of our support as we grow the readership for these amazing works of literature. The more subscribers we have, the more we can demonstrate to potential donors and bookstores alike the diverse support we receive and how we use it to grow our mission in ever-new, ever-innovative ways.

If you would like to get involved with Deep Vellum as a donor, subscriber, or volunteer, please contact us at deepvellum.org. We would love to hear from you.

Thank you all,

Will Evans, Publisher

LIGA DE ORO ($5,000+)

Anonymous (2)

LIGA DEL SIGLO ($1,000+)

Allred Capital Management

Ben Fountain

Judy Pollock

Loretta Siciliano

Lori Feathers

Mary Ann Thompson-Frenk
   & Joshua Frenk

Matthew Rittmayer

Meriwether Evans

Pixel and Texel

Nick Storch

Stephen Bullock

DONORS

Alan Shockley	Christie Tull	Maynard Thomson
Amrit Dhir	Daniel J. Hale	Michael Reklis
Anonymous	Ed Nawotka	Mike Kaminsky
Andrew Yorke	Grace Kenney	Mokhtar Ramadan
Bob Appel	Greg McConeghy	Nikki Gibson
Bob & Katherine Penn	JJ Italiano	Richard Meyer
Brandon Childress	Kay Cattarulla	Suejean Kim
Brandon Kennedy	Kelly Falconer	Susan Carp
Charles Dee Mitchell	Linda Nell Evans	Theater Jones
Charley Mitcherson	Lissa Dunlay	Tim Perttula
Cheryl Thompson	Mary Cline	

SUBSCRIBERS

Adam Hetherington

Adam Rekerdres

Alan Shockley

Alexa Roman

Amber J. Appel

Andrew Lemon

Andrew Strickland

Anonymous

Antonia Lloyd-Jones

Ariel Saldivar

Balthazar Simões

Barbara Graettinger

Ben Fountain

Ben Nichols

Betsy Morrison

Bill Fisher

Bjorn Beer

Bob & Mona Ball

Bob Appel

Bob Penn

Bradford Pearson

Brandon Kennedy

Brina Palencia

Charles Dee Mitchell

Chase LaFerney

Cheryl Thompson

Chris Sweet

Christie Tull

David Hopkins

David Lowery

David Shook

David Weinberger

Dennis Humphries

Dr. Colleen Grissom

Ed Nawotka

Ed Tallent

Elisabeth Cook

Fiona Schlachter

Frank Merlino

George Henson

Gino Palencia

Grace Kenney

Greg McConeghy

Guilty Dave Bristow

Heath Dollar

Horatiu Matei

Jacob Siefring

Jacob Silverman

James Crates

Jane Watson

Jeanne Milazzo

Jeff Whittington

Jeremy Hughes

Joe Milazzo

Joel Garza

John Harvell

Joshua Edwin

Julia Pashin

Julie Janicke Muhsmann

Justin Childress

Kaleigh Emerson

Kenneth McClain

Kimberly Alexander

Lauren Shekari

Linda Nell Evans

Lisa Pon

Lissa Dunlay

Liz Ramsburg

Lytton Smith

Mac Tull

Mallory Davis

Marcia Lynx Qualey

Margaret Terwey

Mark Larson

Martha Gifford

Mary Ann Thompson-Frenk
   & Joshua Frenk

Meaghan Corwin

Michael Holtmann

Mike Kaminsky

Naomi Firestone-Teeter

Neal Chuang

Nicholas Kennedy

Nick Oxford

Nikki Gibson

Owen Rowe

Patrick Brown

Peter McCambridge

Regina Imburgia

Scot Roberts

Sean & Karen Fitzgerald

Shelby Vincent

Steven Norton

Susan Ernst

Taylor Zakarin

Tess Lewis

Tim Kindseth

Todd Mostrog

Tom Bowden

Tony Fleo

Will Morrison

Will Vanderhyden